D0578612

Dear Reader,

Arabesque first launched the AT YOUR SERVICE series, fictional stories of courageous military heroes and heroines, in the summer of 2003. The first title was *Top-Secret Rendezvous* by Linda Hudson-Smith, followed by Candice Poarch's *Courage Under Fire,* followed by *The Glory of Love* by Kim Louise and finally *Flying High* by Gwynne Forster, which wrapped up in 2003. In 2004 the series continued with *Fearless Hearts* by Linda Hudson-Smith, and in 2005 with Courtni Wright's *Windswept Love.*

The AT YOUR SERVICE romance series tells the story of the lives of men and women in the military, and their love…filled with patriotism, camaraderie, romance, passion and intrigue! Every novel draws you in, and you come to appreciate these heroes, as well as the commitment of the people they care about. The series is a fictional account meant to capture the essence of those serving our country, and as such we have taken creative license with the cover photography and the stories we know you will enjoy.

We began planning this unique series honoring African-Americans serving in the military in the spring of 2002, not anticipating the events that would unfold in Iraq.

Now, more than ever, we hope that you enjoy this latest installment of the AT YOUR SERVICE series, *Blue Skies,* by bestselling author Adrianne Byrd. We welcome your comments and feedback, and invite you to send us an e-mail at www.kimanipress.com.

Enjoy,

Evette Porter
Editor
Arabesque Books

Blue Skies

Adrianne Byrd

ARABESQUE®

BLUE SKIES

An Arabesque novel

ISBN-13: 978-0-373-83012-1
ISBN-10:   0-373-83012-2

www.kimanipress.com

Printed in U.S.A.

This book is dedicated to my military fathers:
Robert Saulsbery and Charles Byrd

I miss you both

Prologue

Sunday, August 18, 1982: 1300 hours

"Daddy's not coming home."

Seven-year-old Sydney Garrett lost count of how many times she spoke the words, but she was determined to keep saying them until the girl in the mirror believed it. Really, it didn't make sense. Her father had promised he would come back and everyone knew Lieutenant Colonel Devin Garrett *always* kept his promises.

"Daddy's not coming home."

There was a knock at the door. When Sydney turned, her twelve-year-old brother, Steven, poked his head into the room. He, too, was dressed in his best church clothes and looking as sad as everyone else in the house. Since they'd heard the news, Steven had taken it in his head to start pretending to be the man of the house. Honestly, he wasn't all that good at it, but she would never tell him. Plus, she suspected he already knew.

"You ready?" he asked.

She was and she wasn't. Instead of answering, she dropped her gaze to her shiny black shoes.

Her brother sighed and entered the room. "Uncle Billy says the limousine is on the way and we need to be downstairs when it arrives."

Tears swelled in Sydney's eyes and she quickly blinked them dry. She was a big girl and big girls didn't cry. At least that's what her father had told her, but her mother cried all the time now, and she was definitely a big girl.

But soldiers don't cry.

Steven looped his arm around her shoulders, but she shoved it off and raced from her room.

"Syd," he shouted after her.

She ignored him and raced down the hall to her father's private study. Once inside, she locked the door and backed away. Maybe if she stayed here, she wouldn't have to go. Sydney kept her eyes on the doorknob as she continued to back away from it, her chest heaving as though she'd run the entire backyard a bazillion times.

She bumped into something hard and swiveled around to stare through tear-glazed eyes at her father's desk. On it stood an old, grainy, brown-and-white photo of her grandfather, Tuskegee Airman Lieutenant Anthony Garrett. More tears leaked from her eyes and she drew no comfort from the knowledge her father and grandfather were now together in heaven.

Anger rushed through her body, but she couldn't bring herself to sweep all her father's beloved Second World War model planes to the floor. Instead she took pride in the fact that she knew the difference between the American fighters Grumman F4F Wildcat and the P-51 Mustang, and even the difference between American bombers SB2C and the B-29 Super Fortress—the one that had dropped the atomic bomb.

She knew them all by heart because her father knew them.

She loved them because her father loved them.

A soft knock sounded at the door.

"Sydney?" her mother's voice trembled from the other side. "Honey, it's time to go."

I don't want to go. She turned, dropped to her knees and crawled underneath her father's desk. From there she inhaled the strong wood scent of her father's homemade furniture and the carpet that held the smoky fragrance of his evening cigars.

"Sydney, open the door," her mother coaxed patiently, and then added, "I miss him, too—we all do."

Sydney's tears poured like a waterfall. No one missed him more than she did. No one.

"You know, sweetie." Her mother sniffed. "Your father would want you…us to be strong right now. We have a duty…"

Duty. Her father had spoken the word often, along with others like *honor, courage* and *integrity.*

Sydney took another swipe at her tears. She heard a key rattle in the lock. She pulled her knees up and tucked them beneath her chin. When the door inched open, she wrapped her small arms around herself and transformed into a tight ball—a tight, trembling ball.

Her mother's smooth legs, thin ankles and black shoes entered the room.

Sydney shook her head but no longer made an attempt to silence her sobs. They couldn't make her go if she didn't want to. They couldn't.

Her mother's long legs folded slowly until both knees kissed the carpet. Her mother's head appeared framing her soft, sad brown eyes.

"Sydney, baby. Please come out."

Despite the eyes, everything else about her mother appeared cool, calm and collected. Her mother was beautiful—everyone said so, and today was no exception. If anything, she was more beautiful.

If her father were here he would tell her so.

Sydney dropped her gaze when she thought she saw disappointment flicker across her mother's features.

"I can't do this without you," her mother confessed. "I can't stand at that funeral and pretend to be strong."

"P-pretend?" Sydney eyed her mother wearily.

Her mother nodded, and a part of her cool composure thawed before Syd's eyes.

"I want so very much to get undressed and crawl back into bed and cry forever, but I know in my heart your father wouldn't want that." She smiled as though she remembered something. "Your father used to say my tears broke his heart."

"H-he told me that, too." Sydney sniffed and this time succeeded in drying her face. She didn't want to break her father's heart, but she still didn't want to go to the funeral.

When Syd made no move to crawl out from under her father's desk, her mother's composure continued to thaw. "Sometimes, honey," she began, "we have to do things we don't want to, but we always have to do the *right* thing."

Mother's and daughter's gazes locked.

"Do you remember what your father used to tell you about doing the right thing?"

Sydney nodded. Her father was a soldier twenty-four hours a day. He lived by the code and died by the…

More tears blurred her eyes and then rolled down her face, but thoughts of her father's heart breaking made her erase them. Big girls don't cry. *Soldiers don't cry.*

How many times had she told her father she wanted to be an airman just like him—and Grandpa? She closed her eyes and remembered how his smile grew whenever she told him that.

"You'll make a great airman!" He pulled her pigtail and winked.

Sydney drew a deep breath and thrust up her chin. "I won't cry," she murmured, opening her eyes.

Her mother's tears had now worn a visible track through her makeup.

Sydney forced a smile and then crawled out from her hiding place. "I'm ready to go now."

Pride glimmered in her mother's eyes as she pulled herself up from the floor. Before heading out of the study, her mother pulled a compact from her black purse and fixed her makeup. Once the damage was repaired, she smiled down.

"You look beautiful, Momma."

"Thank you, baby." She took Sydney's hand and led her out the door. They joined the rest of the family downstairs just as the limousines arrived.

It was a beautiful day. Sydney couldn't remember ever seeing the grass so green, the clouds so white and the sky so blue.

Chapter 1

Major Sydney "Serious" Garrett of the U.S. Air Force 51st Fighter Wing entered through the gates of Osan Air Base and flashed her badge through several checkpoints before parking outside the squadron's building.

A baby-faced young airman in a standard-issue olive-green flight suit greeted her with a salute. "Morning, Major Garrett."

She saluted blithely, wondering if the military were now recruiting straight out of junior high.

"Flying today, Serious?"

Sydney relinquished her thoughts to glance up at the base's vice commander, Colonel Jeff Mickelson. With practiced restraint, she stilled her eyes from rolling, erased every emotion from her face and saluted. "We're all here to do a job, sir."

The statement only caused Mickelson's smile to broaden while he shook his head. "It's always about the j-o-b with you." His lips sloped again. "You know, I don't think the military gods would fault you if every now and then you actually relaxed on your day off."

She said nothing and kept her face blank.

"You know how to relax, don't you?" He stepped closer. "It's when you and a few of your friends—I'm sure you have a couple of those—go to the Officers' Club, mix and mingle. I, for one, would like to know what you actually look like in a dress." His gaze landed on the top of her head. "I'm even curious to see you with your hair down. I'm guessing it hangs past your shoulders." Mickelson paused. "Am I right?"

She swallowed her irritation. "You'd be correct, sir."

He nodded and then considered her. "You're a damn good pilot, Garrett. I'll give you that. And you're *not* the only airman we have that eats, sleeps and breathes our fine military—but you are the only one that I have to *order* to take a day off."

Mickelson made sure their gazes locked. "I'll expect to see you next Saturday at the Officers' Club."

She gulped down another lump of irritation.

"Yes, sir." She saluted again, hoping to end this torture with some shred of dignity.

His expression revealed he knew what she was doing, but he saluted back and stalked off.

Sydney marched in the opposite direction and signed in at the operations desk.

"Surprised to see you here today." Major Brian Mohr's voice dripped with sarcasm.

"Can it," she snapped, not ready for round two. Just because she had to take that crap from a colonel didn't mean she had to take it from another gold-leaf airman.

How anyone could think about partying at some Officers' Club with all the mounting tension with neighboring North Korea was beyond her. Yes, the communist country had been threatening a pre-emptive strike against the United States for nearly twenty years, but judging by the latest intelligence, or intel, seeping from the Pentagon and the White House, those threats were sounding more like promises.

Lessons learned from the 1950 Korean War warned that the country relied on the element of surprise. They had kept on surprising the world in 1994 when they'd openly admitted to secretly developing nuclear weapons—a direct violation of Article IV-1 of their agreement with the Secretary of State.

The problem, however, with North Korea's blatant and ballsy admission was that this country was armed with more than a million soldiers, making it the third-largest army in the world.

The question was no longer *if* the country had nuclear weapons, but *what* they were planning to do with them.

No one talked of the possibilities. The North Korean situation was like the elephant in the United Nations' living room.

Major Mohr briefed Sydney on today's sortie—air mission—near the demilitarized zone or DMZ, which lay between North and South Korea. The DMZ was the area between the North and the South where military activity was not permitted. Today was a standard "two-ship" formation with Sydney as lead pilot and Captain Taylor "Puck" Johnson as her wingman.

She had lost count of how many times she had flown this sortie near the DMZ; it was nothing more than a routine mission.

"Your handle today is Delta 6-6 and Puck's Delta 6-7."

"I'm one shy from the devil's mark," Sydney commented.

"It's a good way to let the enemy know not to mess with you," Mohr said without missing a beat. "Like the rest of us."

The comment wrangled her first smile of the day.

Mohr looked thunderstruck.

"What?" she challenged, a little more defensively than she'd intended.

"Nice smile." He shrugged.

Sydney rolled her eyes. "Let me guess. You'd like to see me in a dress with my hair down, too?"

Mohr's eyebrows rose in amusement. "I honestly don't think my heart could take the shock."

She smiled again and strolled off to the locker room. There, she removed her insignia patches, which were secured to her uniform with Velcro, and slid into her G-suit. If she were to be captured, this would keep the enemy from knowing the name of her unit. Name, rank and serial number was all they would ever get out of her.

Less than thirty minutes later, and after a series of preflight checks, Sydney sat strapped in an F-16D, helmet and oxygen mask on. After she'd given the crew chief the thumbs-up signal, the cockpit ladder was detached and the chocks were removed from the wheels of the plane.

Sydney switched on the power and started the small engine. She took hold of the throttle while the engine roared to life. Her heart pounded with giddy excitement; she was ready for takeoff. It was the same rush she'd always felt, ever since her father had first brought her around planes. She was born to fly. Nothing on earth had ever given her the same exhilaration as blazing through the sky.

That's not true.

A pair of gold-colored eyes twinkled from a memory. She sucked in a breath from the unexpected image and her hand flew to the silver band looped on a chain around her neck.

"Is everything all right, Delta 6-6?"

Nothing ever made it past tower control. "Never better." Minutes later, Sydney was cleared for takeoff and she rolled down the runway at full thrust. Once the afterburner kicked in, she rocketed into the air. The earth, along with its troubles, disappeared beneath her.

Captain James "Jett" Colton watched as the two F-16Ds rocketed up the skyway. Though he was grounded, it didn't stop the rush of adrenaline from coursing through his veins. There was nothing close to the grace or beauty of a jet or viper plane.

Maybe nothing, but certainly someone.

He laughed at the renegade thought, turned, and then continued his march to Colonel Mickelson's office. After a series of salutes and cordial smiles, he was quickly led into Mickelson's office. He entered with a salute and held it while the colonel finished his phone conversation.

"Sandy, I don't care which dress you wear to the brigadier general's party. You look good in everything." Mickelson nodded and rolled his eyes toward the ceiling while Sandy tugged on his ear. "Uh-huh. We'll discuss it later, honey. My new airman just showed up."

There were a few more niceties exchanged before Mickelson terminated the call. "Women." He finally saluted. "Can't live with them, can't live without them. Lucky you never married, Colton. Trust me."

"I married once, sir," Jett informed him and judging by the vice commander's face, this information surprised him.

"Really? I must have missed that bit of intel in your files."

"We've sort of been separated for three years."

Mickelson's expression wrinkled. "How long have you been married?"

Jett coughed. "Three years."

"Where are you from, Colton? Hollywood?"

A genuine smile curved onto Jett's face. "No, sir. I'm a Georgia boy—with Hollywood tendencies."

Mickelson barked a hearty laugh and gestured to a vacant chair. "Have a seat, airman."

Jett complied with the order and held his commanding officer's gaze.

"I hear you're a damn good pilot, Colton."

"Thank you, sir."

"And an equal pain in the ass," the colonel added with narrowed eyes. "We don't tolerate any of that hotshot shit around here. Being a hotshot in Korea will get you killed."

Jett swallowed, held his anger in check and maintained eye contact.

"File says that a pilot error cost our fine military

an eighteen-million-dollar plane in Afghanistan. Is that true?"

"That's what the report states," Jett responded in a clipped voice.

"That's not what I asked you." Mickelson's polished gaze remained leveled.

"In that case, Colonel." Jett straightened in his chair. "No. That report is a load of crap. I believed then, as I do now, that my actions saved lives."

"But cost millions."

"I'm not aware of the cost of a human life—let alone fifty-eight of them—sir."

The air thickened with a palpable tension.

Mickelson's beady eyes felt like a human CT scan and though Jett kept his back straight, his chin up and his eyes level, he couldn't help but wonder what his new base commander saw.

"Well, someone else must think this report is full of it, too, seeing how this 'pilot error' didn't end your career. It also makes me the lucky SOB who gets to take you under my wing."

Jett staved off a smile while another thick layer of tension crammed into the room.

Apparently, Mickelson decided he liked what he saw, and his face split with a wide smile as he stood. "Welcome to Osan." He thrust out his hand over the desk.

"Thank you, sir." Jett stood, as well, and accepted the handshake. "I'm thrilled to be a part of the family."

Mickelson stopped pumping Jett's hand, but didn't release his grip. "Family you may be, but I'll still have my eye on you—make sure you follow the house rules."

"Yes, sir."

Mickelson released his hand. "Dismissed."

Coasting through the crystal-blue sky and bursting through scattered clouds, Sydney almost forgot she was barreling through the sky strapped to high-explosive missiles—almost. She glanced at her center console, double-checked her airspeed, altitude and bearing. To her left the threat-warning system lit up.

She blinked, somehow momentarily unable to register her dire situation. "I've been…"

"Missiles in the air," Puck shouted into the airwaves.

She looked around—couldn't see. What the hell was going on? Then at last, she saw it. A large missile was blasting toward her. Sydney pulled up, trying to outdistance it—an unlikely feat given how close it was on her when she spotted it.

Go toward it.

An unmistakable voice from her past spoke as though he rode shotgun in the cockpit. She ignored the command and proceeded to try to outmaneuver the missile, but no matter what she did, it remained hot on her trail.

Go toward it.

Sydney rocked her wings and caught sight of the missile again. As quickly as she could manage, she readjusted her position and this time headed straight for the missile. This maneuver would cause the missile's obvious heat-seeking capabilities to slow down and wait for her. Once she drew close, she would switch or perform a glide-and-roll in the opposite direction. By then, the missile would be unable to adjust and it would lack the power to speed up again to give chase.

Calm, she stated her position, and timed her maneuver as best as she could. Face-to-face with the missile, Sydney thought her heart was beating outside of her chest, but she was determined and focused. "Now," she commanded herself, and did a perfect glide-and-roll. However, there was more than one missile airborne.

The second missile slammed into her. In the next nanosecond, smoke billowed into the cockpit and flames licked all around her. "I'm hit!" She coughed, choked and felt for the ejection handle.

Ejecting out of a jet wasn't as textbook as it sounded. It was more or less something a pilot read about, but only an elite few ever put it to practice…and lived to tell the tale.

Fear stalled her hand for another nanosecond. Would it work? Would she slam into something and become paralyzed? One thing was for sure, if she did nothing, she, along with her plane, would become a blazing fireball long before it hit the ground.

Whispering a prayer, Major Sydney Garrett pulled the handle and ejected...somewhere over North Korea.

Chapter 2

All hell broke loose at Osan Air Base.

Jett had just opened the door to his car when the base went on full alert. Soldiers peeled out of buildings and squadrons to race to unknown destinations. His heart kicked up a notch as adrenaline rushed through his veins.

Still standing with his car door wide open, he caught sight of Colonel Mickelson marching out of the building as if the devil himself chewed at his heels. A soldier for more than half his life, Jett was ready to spring into action—but technically he wasn't a part of the team until tomorrow. He hadn't even met his direct commanding officer. Never a bystander, Jett closed his car door and followed the crowd of airmen.

Entering a squadron building for the 51st Fighter Wing, Jett melted into the crowd and picked up small tidbits of what was going down.

"Bastards shot one of our F-16s out of the sky," an airman to his left griped.

"I heard we've lost all radar frequencies," another man said. "Whole damn base is blind. We can't even contact Kunsan."

Although Jett was new to Korea, he certainly recognized the name of the only other air force base in South Korea. But what did the airman mean that the whole base was blind? Before Jett voiced the question, a heavy hand landed on his shoulder.

"Aren't you in the wrong area?"

Jett turned toward a gigantically tall, gold-leaf, African-American airman, and quickly saluted. "Yes—no—I mean, I don't know, sir." He cringed at how much of an idiot he sounded.

Major Brian Mohr, according to his name tag, frowned before he returned Jett's salute. "Well, which is it, Captain—" He read Jett's name tag as well. "Captain James Colton." Now his eyes narrowed. "Colton," he repeated. "Why do I know that name?"

"I'm new to the base, sir. When the alarm sounded, I simply followed the running men, sir."

Mohr was already nodding his head halfway through Jett's explanation.

"Your patch identifies you as a member of the re-established Black Knights."

"Affirmative, sir."

Mohr eyed him a second longer and then said, "The 21st Special Operation Squadron is on the other side of the base. Lieutenant Colonel Nick Bradley is your C.O."

Jett nodded and, given his obviously unwelcome reception, retreated.

Mohr snapped his fingers. "You're the hotshot everyone has been talking about, aren't you?"

"I don't pay too much attention to idle talk." Jett kept his face passive though his chest swelled with pride.

Mohr seemed to read straight through him. "You're not in my squadron, Captain Colton. But I'll let you in on a little secret…being a hotshot in Korea—"

"Will get me killed," Jett repeated Mickelson's words and was unable to keep sarcasm from dripping into his tone.

Meanwhile Mohr went from looking mildly annoyed to downright pissed as he stepped forward. "That's right, Captain Colton. It *will* get you killed. A few minutes ago, this air base lost Major Garrett, one of our finest jet pilots."

Jett's chest tightened. "Garrett?"

Mohr's features softened. "You know her?"

Her? Jett swallowed. He wasn't feeling like his normal brave, take-no-prisoners self.

"Major Sydney Garrett. Guys call her—"

"Serious," Jett answered for him again. He knew her handle because he'd been the one who had given it to her years ago. Long before they'd parted ways, long before he fell in love with her—and long before they were married.

Sydney couldn't catch her breath as she plummeted thousands of feet through the sky. Her panic was held in check by years of training and discipline. The scrap metal that had once been a fifteen-million-dollar Prince of the Sky tumbled away from her faster, until it became a glowing ball of fire.

Though she was the poster child for training and discipline, Sydney hadn't performed a textbook ejection—but at least she was still alive.

For now.

Tumbling out of control, miles above the earth, still strapped to her ejected seat, Sydney's thoughts slowed down so she could make sense of the jumbled words. And worse, her shock gave way to pain. *Severe* pain.

She hadn't felt it before, but she now remembered the fire in the cockpit, its flames licking at her face. And now the cold air raked at her exposed skin like a cat-o'-nine-tails.

She wouldn't know the extent of her injuries until she reached the ground.

If she reached the ground alive.

Right now, she prayed her parachute would operate once she reached fourteen thousand feet and her ejected seat would fall away. Just as the textbook said it would.

What if it doesn't open?

She glanced around, trying to note her surroundings, but unable to notice anything other than the long green carpet of earth rushing to meet her. Fear reminded her of the toggle switch on her seat pan that would send out a distress signal. A complete rag doll in the wind, Sydney braced herself to accept death.

But there is so much I still want—

She forced herself not to finish the thought. However, she had no control of the images flashing though her mind: the first time she'd touched a jet plane on her father's air base, her father's funeral, marching at the Air Force Academy, her first day at flight school, graduating at the top the class, making airman of the year three years running, her first assignment to Special Operations School…meeting the love of her life.

She squeezed her eyes tight. Surely, she'd reached fourteen thousand feet by now. Where was her damn parachute?

Manic, Sydney reached for the seat handle, but before she could pull, she heard a muffled *pop*. The drogue chute stabilized and slowed her speed. In the next second a louder pop literally brought tears to her eyes as her main parachute bloomed overhead and her seat and headrest fell away.

Sydney snatched off her helmet and oxygen mask and tossed them into the wind. Dizzy from the high altitude, she offered a prayer of thanks to her guardian angel.

However, looking back down at the forest-green carpet she was hit with another concern—trees.

Though it felt as though she'd been falling forever, in truth it had been no more than a few seconds since she had ejected.

And for the first time, Sydney's thoughts returned to her wingman. Where was Captain Johnson? Had he seen her eject from her aircraft?

Her eyes scanned the area above, seeing nothing but blue sky and billowy white clouds. Sydney strained her ears to hear the roar of a jet plane—but only the hard rush of air pounded her eardrums. Had he been hit, as well? Was he out searching for her?

Once she reached the ground, how long would it be before NATO sent in a search and rescue? Of course, that depended on whether the Guard Channel had picked up her distress signal. If not, they would figure she went down with her plane.

Of course, the enemy could pick up her signal, as well—particularly whomever had launched the surface-to-air missiles.

She didn't want to think about that.

The trees grew larger and Sydney reached for the

red handles above her head that were attached to the parachute. This handy doodad helped manipulate the shape of her parachute and aided in steering— but there was nowhere to steer to, no *safe* place to land. One tree would hurt just as much as the next.

If by chance she survived the trees, would hostile forces then meet her? The last time she'd checked, launching a missile at someone wasn't exactly meant as a friendly greeting.

Every Hollywood torture scene she'd ever seen in a darkened theater flooded her mind, doing nothing to calm her anxiety. Her mind raced over the items in her survival kit and vest.

Two-way radio—check.

Global Positioning Satellite—check.

9-mm semiautomatic Beretta pistol—check.

All her training had prepared her for this moment and she was determined to make her country proud.

She kept her eyes glued to the horizon, her legs and feet together, knees bent. For the third time that day, a pair of golden eyes twinkled back at her and the fluttering in her heart was different this time.

Jett.

All too soon, her vision was obscured and merciless tree branches ripped and tore at her and the paper-thin nylon parachute. She tried to reel away, but when something sharp hit the back of her head, the world went black.

Soaring through time…

Chapter 3

Sydney shielded her eyes from the bright Georgia sun as she stepped out of her brother's car. As usual the southern state's humidity made the simple act of breathing an exhausting cardio workout. All in all, it was good to be home.

Henderson's airport really should have been named Henderson's air*strip* because it was just that small. For all intents and purposes it looked like nothing more than a mom-and-pop operation. How had her brother even found this place?

"I can't wait until you see this little baby." Steven's

already wide smile slid even wider as he uncurled his six-foot-six frame out of the car. "She's perfect."

Sydney drew in a deep breath and tried not to roll her eyes skyward, but her next words still had a way of damping her brother's mood. "Are you sure you want to spend two point seven million dollars to buy a Cessna jet?"

"Oh, yeah. This little baby is worth it," he said.

She smiled, nodded and finally rolled her eyes. Steven, who'd had the good fortune to make his millions before the dot-commers went bust, pretty much spent his days as a carefree playboy.

In the military, she got her daily fix of roaring through the sky. Her brother, who wanted nothing to do with the military, had to sate his flying addiction in other ways—at the moment in two point seven million ways.

"Mr. Garrett!" a voice thundered from behind them.

Sydney and Steven turned toward a silver-haired gentleman with skin the color of a lobster. Not everyone can tan.

"Mr. Henderson!" Steven shouted. His mood brightened.

Sydney eyed the two men and knew both were about to engage in a good round of haggling.

"So who's this pretty lady you brought with you?" Mr. Henderson removed his mirrored glasses and flashed steel-gray eyes at her. "Or maybe *beautiful* is the right word?"

Embarrassment burned Sydney's cheeks as she smiled and slid her hand into Henderson's offered one. Accepting compliments for anything other than her flying skills wasn't her strong suit. Today was a rare day: Sydney wore a white summer dress and allowed her thick hair to hang loose.

"This is my sister," Steven replied, rocking on his heels. "I brought her to get her professional opinion."

Henderson's brows shot up with surprise. "*She's* the F-16 fighter pilot you were bragging about?" His incredulity heightened his comic-book features.

"She knows her stuff," Steven bragged and puffed out his chest. "I figured I'd bring her out to get her professional opinion of the plane."

Henderson gave her another cursory yet calculating glance before he released her hand. "Well, it's certainly nice to meet you. When I was in the military we didn't have women as beautiful as you working on the front lines...of course, there were plenty of gorgeous Nightingales in the hospitals. I even managed to marry one." He winked.

"Lucky you," she said, barely able to contain her sarcasm.

Steven pierced her with his "behave" look and Sydney simply ignored him.

"Matt!" a man yelled out the door of the white airport hub.

The small group all turned toward the loud man. "Telephone!"

Henderson waved to let the young man know that he'd heard him and then turned back toward Steven and Sydney. "That should be the bank. Why don't we go inside and do a little business?"

"I haven't decided to sign on the dotted line yet," Steven warned.

"You will." Henderson patted his back. "You will." Henderson swung an arm around her brother's shoulders.

"We'll see." Steven glanced at Sydney. "You want to come in?"

"I'll just wait around out here," Sydney said, flashing her best smile.

"Don't sign anything until you take me on a test flight," she reminded him.

Henderson squeezed Steven's shoulders. "This shouldn't take long."

Once the men disappeared into the building, Sydney sighed and glanced around the small airport, bored.

"What a beautiful afternoon," she mumbled under her breath, and then leaned back on the hood of her brother's car and turned her face up toward the sky and imagined herself soaring.

A car's engine roared behind her while gravel crunched beneath tires, but Sydney wasn't willing to abandon her daydreaming to see who was pulling into the airport. The car stopped next to her and the engine shut off seconds before the car door opened.

It was probably the ensuing silence that finally piqued her curiosity and she opened her eyes.

Sydney sucked in an involuntary breath when her gaze met eyes the color of fresh honey and a smile that rivaled the sun. She blinked, certain that the image would disappear once she opened her eyes again.

No such luck.

"I wasn't sure you were real, either," he said with a soft chuckle.

She swallowed and pretended the man's warm, seductive voice wasn't strumming her heartstrings.

"Jett Colton." He thrust out a hand and continued to blind her with his smile.

"Jett?"

"It's my call sign."

"Call sign?" she feigned ignorance.

"Yeah. I'm an air force fighter pilot. My friends call me Jett because I like anything fast." His gaze was unwanted but still felt as good as a lover's caress.

"Good for you." Sydney's eyes lowered to his hand, but she didn't dare take it. Her entire body was setting off warning alarms and for the first time in her life her heart was vulnerable to a stranger's invasion.

"O-o-okay." Jett relaxed his arm back at his side as his next chuckle sounded more like a misfired weapon. "You don't talk much." He eyed her bare fingers. "I don't see a ring—so you're not married. And being as beautiful as you are, if you don't already have a man on the hook, you must have a few fish swarming toward it."

Sydney rolled her eyes. Why were all the good-looking ones dumb as hell?

Jett crossed his arms and leaned back against his own car and studied her.

"Why are you doing that?"

"Doing what?" he asked with convincing innocence.

"Staring at me."

"Because you're beautiful."

Another heat wave scorched her face. "Thanks—but stop it. It's…rude."

Jett laughed, seemingly oblivious to the fact that she hadn't joined him. "So what's the deal? You're not married and you don't have a boyfriend—"

"I didn't say I didn't have a boyfriend."

His eyebrows crashed together. "Do you?"

"Well…no."

"Good."

"I just don't like you," she lied.

Jett's smile disappeared as though she'd slapped him. After a few strained heartbeats, his lips bloomed wider than before. "Liar."

The man's response was so incredible—so unexpected, that Sydney's laughter burst out before she had a chance to contain it.

Jett pushed off from his car and moved closer to her. "Please tell me that you like a man who makes you laugh."

"You don't give up, do you?" she asked, still amused. He moved so close that the day's slight breeze flapped her dress against his pant legs.

"Tell me you find a man who goes after what he wants a complete turn-on."

Sydney's amusement evaporated and those alarm warnings came in loud and clear.

"Tell me you like a man who seeks only to please—both body and soul."

Jett's last word blew like a breeze across her cheek and her knees weakened. "You're good," she whispered. "Cheesy but good."

Jett's brows arched. "You're not half bad yourself."

She wanted to sidestep him or push him back to allow herself more breathing room, but both options would require that she touch him, and judging by her body's warning system, that was not an option.

"You want to go up?" he asked, snapping her out of her trance.

"Up?"

"A trip up into the great blue wonder." He tilted his head up to the sky. "I'm a pretty good pilot. I promise to keep you safe."

The man's beautiful eyes were having a vertigo effect on her. It was the only way to describe the sensation of falling.

"What do you say?" he continued. "Are you up for the challenge?"

Sydney swallowed and gained control of her fast-beating heart through the steel discipline of her military training. When she felt like herself again, she met his leveled gaze. "Challenge accepted."

Chapter 4

Sydney slid into the leather seats of a brand-new '99 Cessna Piper N226T and resisted the urge to run her hand over the controls.

"Make sure you buckle up," Jett said, entering through the pilot's door and winking. "I have to protect the precious cargo."

Sydney smiled, shook her head and reached for the seat belt. It was a good thing this guy was good-looking, because he was growing cheesier by the moment.

"It seems I have a knack for putting a smile on your face," he commented, shutting his door.

"That you do," she admitted.

"Seems to me it's as good a reason as any to tell me your name."

Her gaze swept up to his mesmerizing stare and she tried to deny his crooked smile had anything to do with the knots looping in her stomach. "Syd," she croaked, and then cleared her throat. "Sydney Garrett."

"Sydney." He tried the name out and rolled his eyes as if he were pondering some great theological quagmire. "Sydney," he repeated.

The strange thing was she sort of liked how his seductive timbre caressed her name while he weighed his decision.

Finally, he turned to her and nodded. "I like it."

"I'll make sure I tell my mother."

Laughing, Jett placed the headphones over his ears and spoke with the control tower.

Sydney turned her head, but her gaze remained locked on the handsome pilot while she enjoyed the light fluttering in her stomach. A voice in her head questioned what she was doing, several times in fact, but damned if she had an answer—and damned if she could pull her eyes away from Jett.

As if sensing her gaze, Jett glanced back at her and winked without stopping the flow of conversation with the control tower. "Roger that," he said into the headset and started the plane. The plane's propellers twirled to life and the loud hum of the engine filled her veins with that familiar anxious anticipation she loved.

"Nervous?" Jett asked, misreading her expression.

"Hardly," she responded, unable to keep her smile from spreading wider across her face.

His expression turned curious, but instead of questioning her, he taxied the aircraft toward the runway.

Sydney's heart raced as they headed down the long cement strip and then, at takeoff, it soared.

"That's my girl," Jett crooned under his breath and then cast a sly glance in her direction. "A good plane is like a good woman." He winked.

"Oh, really?" Her brows quirked at the international line male pilots used to hook unsuspecting women.

"Really." Jett pulled back on the steering and the plane climbed higher in the clouds. "If you respect them and take good care of them, they'll respond to your slightest touch." He gently pushed the throttle and the plane leveled off.

She had hoped to keep a straight face through the cheesy line, however, the task proved impossible and her head rocked as laughter burst from her lungs.

"What?" he asked, a knowing smile curling his lips.

"What did you do, memorize a book of campy pick-up lines?" she asked, not bothering to rein in her amusement.

"That wasn't a line."

"Right. And neither is 'My friends call me Jett because I like anything fast.'" She shook her head.

"I think I would have liked you better if you came up to me, scratched your balls, clubbed me on the back of the head and dragged me back to your cave."

Sidney kept her nose high in the air while she folded her arms, but as their gazes held, she worried about the growing amusement in Jett's eyes. Finally, when his lips curled upward, he switched to auto-pilot and started to move out of his chair.

"Where are you going?" Syd asked, unconcerned about the plane, but suspicious about the pilot.

"To see whether I have a club somewhere."

His Boy Scout expression and his answer wrangled a laugh from her and she shook her head. "Point, match, game."

Laughing along with her, Jett leaned back in his seat and removed his headphones. "Well, Ms. Garrett, how are you enjoying your flight so far?"

More knots looped in her stomach while she languished beneath Jett's magnetic gaze. No way was she going to fall for his mile-high Casanova move the way, undoubtedly, so many women before her had succumbed.

"It's not a difficult question," Jett said with more than a fair dose of amusement.

Her smile returned. "So far, so good." She faced him again, mainly because he fascinated her. "At best I can say you're a fairly competent pilot."

His eyebrows crept to the center of his forehead. "You know about flying?"

"I know a little sumpthin' sumpthin'. There are a few pilots in my family. The blue skies are like my second home."

She could tell her answer surprised him and she noticed for the first time the lone dimple in his right cheek when he smiled.

"Maybe we should start over," he said, lifting a hand. "James Colton."

Sydney hesitated and then slid her hand into his massive one. Nothing could prepare her for the volts of electricity his touch charged into her, but she could feel every atom in her body respond to him. Judging by his expression, he knew his effect and reveled in it.

Suddenly, and quite unexpectedly, the plane jerked once, twice and then one propeller slowed— and then the other.

"Damn." Jett turned around in his seat and jerked his headphones back onto his head. "Not now."

"Not now? This has happened before?" she asked, and then gripped the sides of her seat when the plane dived forward.

"The engine stalled," he said as casually as giving her the time.

The comment wasn't necessary. Sydney knew exactly what was going on; she just wanted to know what he was going to do about it.

Jett tried to restart the engine, but each time, his efforts were met with an eerie silence.

"C'mon, baby. C'mon, baby," he coocd and co-erced the plane.

"Here, let me try," Sydney offered, already reaching for her seat buckle.

"I got it. I got it," he answered without sparing a glance in her direction. Meanwhile, the plane continued to plummet like a stone.

Sydney ignored him and unlocked her seat belt, completely prepared to shove Jett out of the pilot seat if need be. However, the moment she pulled out of her seat, the plane's engine roared to life. The aircraft jerked violently in reaction and pitched Sydney to the back of the plane.

She hit the back wall headfirst and literally had to blink stars from her eyes.

Jett glanced over his shoulder. "Are you all right?"

Sydney opened her mouth to respond, but instead a large wave of laughter rolled out.

He stole another look over his shoulder.

Despite sensing genuine concern in his expression and knowing there was nothing funny about their miniemergency, Sydney couldn't cork her laughter.

"Should I have ground control have the paramedics on hand when we land?" he questioned.

She shook her head and wiped a few errant tears from her eyes. "I—I'm fine," she lied. Her head hurt like hell and she was convinced regaining any sort of equilibrium would qualify as a miracle.

However, her laughter kept rolling as she stumbled back toward the front of the plane.

"Maybe I should have the local psych ward meet us with a straitjacket?"

His eyes twinkled again while his lone dimple made another dramatic appearance and Sydney's stomach found room for one more knot to loop. "I may agree to that seeing as how I let you talk me onto this flying death trap."

She plopped unceremoniously back into her seat and strapped on her seat belt.

Jett's head rocked back with a hearty laugh, the sound of which caused goose bumps to pimple her body.

"What do you say I make it up to you?"

"How do you make up for almost killing someone?"

His shoulders hiked while his smile spread wide. "Dinner?"

Sydney shook her head and emitted a soft chuckle. She struggled to be casual because dating had never been one of her strong suits. Men generally thought she was too rigid and too serious, which was probably true since all she ever talked about was the military and, of course, flying.

"Come on, I promise I won't bite."

She glanced over and had an idea of the temptation Eve had endured in the Garden of Eden. Like her great foremother, Sydney felt herself weakening beneath his golden gaze.

"Of course, if you're afraid—"

"I'm not afraid of you."

The intensity of Jett's eyes nearly melted the clothes off her body. "No boyfriend. No husband. What's wrong with you then?"

The question caught her off guard and she instantly grew defensive. "What makes you think there something wrong with me?"

"It's obvious." He chuckled with another hike to his shoulders. "A beautiful, intelligent woman like you should have easily hooked a husband by now. The only reason I can think this hasn't happened is because you're some kind of black widow."

Sydney's brows shot up on that one.

"You know, the kind that kills their mate." Jett jiggled his eyebrows.

The plane jerked again.

"You should talk."

The runway came into view and Jett informed the tower of their approach for landing. "So was that a yes?" he asked Sydney.

She hesitated again, still uncertain and uncomfortable with her body's mutinous response to him. As a military airman—or airwoman—she was unaccustomed to this feeling of being out of control. It scared her...and thrilled her at the same time.

"You, me—dinner? What do you say?"

Don't do it. "All right." She drew a deep breath and gagged the little voice in her head. "It's a date."

Chapter 5

The excitement about his date with the very lovely Sydney Garrett waned the moment Jett turned down the street toward his childhood home. In its place a jittering anxiety thinned his breath and his hand tightened on the steering wheel.

He'd grown up in Atlanta, but he never thought of the place as home. With no memory of his mother and a father who had been alcoholic and abusive, Jett's only refuge was his older brother, Xavier.

His brother couldn't always save him, even though Xavier was their father's favorite. What Gerald Colton hadn't counted on was that the moment his golden child turned eighteen, he would leave Georgia and never look back.

Jett, on the other hand, found himself returning frequently for more abuse. In the beginning, he came back to prove to his father that he'd been wrong about him. That he wasn't worthless. The plan never worked. Now, he didn't know why he kept returning.

A successful and decorated fighter pilot after his tour in Iraq ended, he made sure that a third of his check was sent home, despite his suspicion that his father just drank through the money. No appreciation. No gratitude. No nothing.

And here he was ready for more abuse.

Jett drove up the cracked cement driveway and cut off his car's engine. He didn't immediately climb out of the car. Instead, he continued to prepare himself for what awaited him this time.

Bethany Garrett opened her front door and gasped in surprise at seeing her daughter. "Sydney," she squealed as she threw her arms out wide and embraced her youngest child. Her joy heightened at the rare sight of Sydney wearing a dress.

"Let me take a good look at you." Bethany stepped back and fluttered a hand over her heart. More often than not, it had seemed that she and her late husband had had two boys as opposed to a boy and a girl.

Sydney smiled as she performed a perfect pirouette. "I thought you might like this." When she finished, she ran a hand through her roller-curled locks to point out that her hair was not swept back into its usual tight bun.

Her mother's eyes glossed with tears. "Oh, my. How pretty you look. I'm almost afraid to ask what's the occasion."

"No occasion. I just wanted to surprise you and invite you on a girls' day out."

Her mother's eyes grew wider as she clapped her hands together. "Shopping? You're actually going to go shopping with me?"

To Sydney, she looked like a little child who had just been granted a Christmas wish. "Yeah, Mom. I'm a woman for a day." She placed a finger against her lips. "Shh. Don't tell anybody."

"Excuse me. Coming through," Steven announced, shouldering his way into the house with Sydney's bags.

"You knew that she was coming and kept it from me?" Bethany playfully slapped her son's arm.

"Had to. I was threatened with bodily harm." He leaned over and planted a kiss on his mother's upturned cheek.

"In that case, I forgive you."

Steven's smile beamed before he bounded up the stairs to deliver Sydney's luggage to her old bedroom.

Bethany laughed then grabbed hold of Sydney for another hug. "Ooh, why didn't you call and tell me?" She pulled back and removed her enormous floppy sunhat. "I've been digging out in the garden. I'll need to shower, change and call your uncle—"

"Uncle Billy?" Sydney frowned, and then tried to remember the last time she had actually spoken to her uncle. "Why do you have to call him?"

"He's in town, too. On leave, he said." Her mother rushed up the staircase with her hand still locked on Sydney's wrist. It was almost as if she feared that if she let go, Sydney would vanish.

"If you already have other plans—"

"No plans," her mother tossed over her shoulder. "He and some pilot friend of his are gallivanting through town and I was actually in the middle of trying to beg them to come over for dinner—maybe catch the fireworks downtown. You know your uncle—he's always too busy."

Sydney smiled, though she detected hurt in her mother's voice. She suspected that her uncle Billy avoided the family for other reasons. Like he didn't want to be around people who reminded him of his beloved brother—of what he had lost.

"Well, we're going have a great time shopping," Sydney proclaimed. Usually she found such outings a bore, but seeing as how she had impulsively agreed to a date without having packed for such an occasion, she needed to shop.

"What we have to do is mark this day in history," Steven said, coming out of her room. "You agreeing to date someone you haven't performed a ten-point inspection on. It's a miracle."

"A date?" Her mother perked up and clapped her hands together. "I'm so..." she searched for a long time before coming up with the word "...proud."

Sydney's eyebrows clashed together. "Proud?"

Steven reeled with laughter.

"Shut up, Steven."

Her mother shook her head and then slid an arm around Sydney's shoulders. "Well, I'm just saying that you—you know, you don't go on too many of those. Dates, I mean."

Sydney patiently folded her arms. "For your information, Afghanistan isn't exactly a singles' hotspot."

"Yes, yes. You're right, dear." Bethany stole another hug. "I'm sorry, baby. C'mon on in here while I get ready and you can tell me all about your new boyfriend."

"He's not my boyfriend."

"Yet, dear." Her mother winked. "He's not your boyfriend yet."

"You mean he hasn't been home in the last three days?" Jett asked Mrs. Stewart, his father's neighbor for twenty years. "Did you call the police or anyone?"

Mrs. Stewart twisted her weathered face in disapproval. "Now, chile. I keep to myself. You know I make it a point not to stick my nose in anyone's business."

He nodded along with the lie in hopes she'd just spill the beans as to why the house was trashed and his father was M.I.A.

"Besides," Mrs. Stewart went on. "The cops are tired of people always calling about Gerald. If he's not stumbling drunk into other people's yards in the middle of the night or trying to break into the wrong house, he's dragging shady characters into the neighborhood." She tsked under her breath. "Half-dressed women and thugs that can't keep their pants up."

Jett scratched his head and drew in a deep breath. None of this information helped him figure out where to begin his search. When he'd first walked into the house, he'd experienced what it must feel like to wander into the twilight zone.

Tables were overturned, furniture ripped to shreds and almost every square inch of the place was covered in shattered glass. Did his father do it in a drunken rage? Or had his father, once again, gotten himself into something he couldn't get out of?

"Okay, thanks, Mrs. Stewart." He flashed a tight smile and turned away from her door.

"You know, I always thought you were the good one," she said sadly. "You're a good son, looking after your father the way you do."

Jett glanced over his shoulder, feeling more than a little guilty for enjoying her praise.

"God willing, one of these days Gerald's going to realize that." She winked. "I hope you find him."

He nodded and descended the porch steps. *Where to start?* Jett glanced at his watch. He had four hours to find his father before he was to meet Sydney at Hi-Life Café. "I can do this," he coached himself and headed out to search the usual bars and holes in the wall where his father hung out.

Sydney stared at her reflection in her old bedroom mirror and wondered for the umpteenth time why she'd selected the dress. She did like the color, a beautiful powder blue with a modest collar and short sleeves.

Her main concern was with the pencil skirt. She would have to take small steps and keep her knees glued together. However, she did like the way the shape gave the illusion of an hourglass figure.

"Mind if I come in now?" her mother questioned from the other side of the door.

Sydney drew a deep breath. "Sure. C'mon in."

Her mother pushed open the door and immediately gasped at the sight of her. "You look gorgeous," she commented as she swept into the room. "You're positively radiant."

"Thanks, Mom." She felt strange under the glowing praise. These mother-and-daughter moments were rare indeed, considering Sydney's usual wardrobe outside of her air force blues was jeans and a T-shirt.

Sydney turned back toward the mirror. "I was

thinking about pinning up my hair. What do you think?"

"No. No." Her mother fussed as she gave her daughter's curls a light pat. "You always wear it up. It looks so beautiful down."

Sydney nodded but still fretted before her reflection. "You don't think that I'm trying too hard?" She glanced at her mother. "What if I'm overdressed?"

"Nonsense. You look perfect. Stop worrying."

Sydney drew a deep breath to calm her nerves, uncertain what made her so nervous. Jett was handsome—true, but it wasn't as if she hadn't been around good-looking men. The air force was full of them. There was also no shortage of cocky hotshot pilots, either.

So what is it?

She thought it over for a long moment while she smoothed her hand down her dress. Then it came to her. It was his eyes. A beautiful gold that twinkled when he smiled, but they held or maybe hid something else.

"You really like this guy, huh?"

Her mother's question jarred her from her private thoughts and she managed a shaky smile. "I really don't know him, Momma."

"Uh-huh." Her mother winked and then walked out of the room.

Sydney arrived at Hi-Life Café at precisely eight o'clock. She was a little disappointed that her date was late, but she held on to her smile while the waitress showed her to her table.

However, eight o'clock came and went.

So did nine o'clock.

At 2:00 a.m. Jett found his father crumpled in the back alley behind a hole-in-the-wall bar nearly forty miles from home. His investigation, which involved talking to his father's friends, coworkers and drinking buddies, was worthy of a *Columbo* episode. He couldn't believe it—and it pained him to admit it—but he was terrified he wouldn't find his father. By the time Jett found Gerald, he was exhausted.

"What the hell are you doing here?" Gerald croaked as Jett struggled to lift him up. "Where's Xavier?"

Jett rolled his eyes at his father's rancid breath. "He's not here, Pop. Put your arm around my shoulder."

Gerald did as his son instructed, but it didn't stop his obsessive questions about his *favorite* son. To make matters worse, when Jett finally placed his father in the car, he chose that time to empty the rest of his stomach's contents.

"Just great," Jett mumbled. He closed the passenger door and walked to the driver's side, praying for strength. He drove back home with all four windows rolled down and his father fast asleep.

A calm came over him now that his father was

safe. When they made it home, Jett struggled again to get his father out of the car and into the house. Getting the man showered and in bed was nothing less than a miracle.

His heart broke again when he tucked his father into bed.

"What the hell are you doing here?" Gerald smacked his son's hands away from the sheet. "Where is Xavier?"

"He's not here, Pop." Jett persisted and smoothed down the sheet. "Get some sleep."

Gerald yawned and curled up against his pillow. "He's coming back, you know. He's coming back."

"Sure, Pop." Jett leaned over and placed a kiss against his father's forehead. "'Night." He turned and walked quietly out of the room.

After he collapsed in one of the uncluttered armchairs and was finally able to relax, he remembered his date with Sydney. Jett bounced up and dug out his cell phone and the folded piece of paper with her name and number on it. He punched in the number and glanced at his watch. He groaned when he realized it was three-thirty in the morning.

He wasn't surprised when he was transferred to voice mail, but at the sound of the beep, he didn't know what to say.

"Uh—hey, Sydney. It's me—your very, *very* late date. Um, I'm so sorry but, er, something sort of came up and I...well, I sort of forgot about our date and I…I know that sounds lame, but I guess…well, I guess I wanted to apologize. If you could call me when you get this message I would love to explain everything to you." He paused and searched for something else to say, but came up empty. "Okay then. I look forward to hearing from you. Bye."

Jett disconnected the phone and knew within his heart of hearts that Sydney Garrett was never going to call him back. "Goddamn it!"

On the brink of war…

Chapter 6

Bethany Garrett woke from a deep sleep. For a few heartbeats she wasn't sure of what had awakened her, but the telephone's loud shrill caused her heart to leap with fear. No one called her house this time of night unless there was something wrong.

Clicking on the lamp, Bethany jerked up in bed ramrod-straight, but she didn't immediately pick up the receiver. It was almost as if she was momentarily paralyzed with fear. Was it about Steven? Sydney?

As much as she wanted to dismiss this sudden

wave of paranoia, Bethany *knew* something was wrong.

Just before the call transferred to the answering machine, Bethany found the courage to pick up. However, lifting her arm to place the phone against her ear was a slow and arduous chore.

"Hello, Mom? Are you there?"

Her entire body exploded with relief at the sound of her son's voice. Maybe she *was* paranoid. "Steven." She sighed and slouched back against the bed's pillows. "Do you have any idea what time it is?"

"Mom, have you seen the news?"

Bethany noted Steven's agitation and…panic? "Well, no." She glanced around the bed to see if she could spot the remote control to her bedroom's television set.

As it had been since her husband's death, the entire left side of the bed was a neat clutter of books, clothes, newspapers and God knew whatever else. It was a psychological trick not to make the bed seem so empty and she knew it.

"Mom?"

"Yeah, wait. Hold on a second." She spotted the remote atop her latest Michael Connelly novel and jabbed the power button. "It's on. What am I looking for?" Fear crept into her voice.

"CNN," came her son's flat reply.

Bethany punched in the right channel and immediately sucked in her breath when a newsman with a concrete expression stared at her through the television set. But it was the red letters to the right of his head that held her spellbound. North Korea's blue and red flag had a one-word question scrawled diagonally across it: *WAR?*

"No," she croaked. Her mind soared to the last image of Sydney waving goodbye at the glass doors of the Hartsfield-Jackson Airport. Dressed in her military blues, Sydney took great pride in being the embodiment of a United States Air Force fighter pilot. In truth, every time Bethany saw her daughter, her heart broke. She'd never told Sydney this. She'd vowed never to confess her fear of answering her door to see the death angels of the military delivering bad news…again.

She'd never dreamed the news would come from her son over the phone.

Bethany closed her eyes and prayed when she opened them it would be to wake from a nightmare.

"Mom, are you there?"

Steven's voice was all the reality she needed. Her tears didn't require her eyes to open in order to spill down her cheeks.

"Momma?"

"I have to go," she said. "I have to call your sister. I have to see—"

"No calls are getting through." His own voice tumbled over flat notes of despair. "The whole damn country is like it's been wiped…" He drew a breath. "I've been calling different newspapers and news stations and they are all unable to confirm anything. A part of it may be the sixteen-hour time difference."

Try as she might, Bethany couldn't make sense out of what her son was saying or implying. She also didn't want to analyze what the pain ebbing into her heart meant.

"I even tried calling the Pentagon." Anguish seized control of Steven's voice, and his words were punctuated with heartrending sobs. "I—I have a few contacts and I—I—"

"What are they saying?" Bethany asked, though she didn't want to know. She wasn't sure whether she could handle it.

"No one has been able to contact Osan Air Force Base." Steven drew a deep breath and managed to garner some measure of control. "The only base in the region they've been able to contact is Kadena."

"But that's in Japan," Bethany answered, remembering her husband's brief deployment there years ago.

"Kadena is on high alert, maybe even preparing to launch counterattacks—"

"Counterattacks?"

"Maybe—probably. Initial reports are saying Kim Jong-il launched six missiles. A few fell into the Sea of Japan. It's believed North Korea is finally going to deliver on its promise."

"And Sydney is right in the middle of it."

"I'm afraid so."

Jett didn't know what was happening to him. Everything moved in slow motion and he felt as if he'd been submerged at the bottom of the ocean and the only sound that filled his ears was his own heartbeats.

He didn't remember walking out of the hangar or even returning to his car. Yet, he didn't return to his new quarters or even turn the engine over. All he did, all he seemed *able* to do, was sit.

Jett waited—for the pain, the tears and the denial—but nothing came. He just felt…numb. What did that mean? He loved Sydney. Even after all this time, that hadn't changed.

He remembered in vivid detail the first day he'd laid eyes on her. She was leaning back against a car, her face tilted toward the sky. Nothing before or since had ever looked more beautiful. When she opened her deep, sable-colored eyes, his heart tugged, pinched and tried to squeeze out of his chest. It was as if it recognized its other half—its better half.

They were like oil and water from the start. Sydney's beauty captured his attention, but it was her fire and downright take-no-crap attitude that had him hook, line and sinker….

Our love…

Chapter 7

Crisp in his air force blues, Jett marched beneath the blazing sun. He took special note of the other men marching before him and drew his measure. The best of the best from the navy and air force all marched before him. Adrenaline pumped through his veins and accelerated his heart at the thought of flying and competing against them. He couldn't wait for the rest of them to discover what he already knew.

He was the best.

When he'd learned of his selection for the Weapon

School tactical training program there was satisfaction in knowing that despite his so-called hotshot tendencies, the powers that be knew what they had in him.

Upon entering the appointed classroom, Jett chose a seat near the back. It was the perfect bird's-eye view of everything and everyone. In minutes, the room was filled nearly to capacity and the instructors had begun to filter in from a door in front of the classroom.

Then something happened. The atmosphere changed. The room's atoms shifted—something. Whatever it was, Jett was suddenly compelled to glance toward the main door. What he saw shocked the hell out of him.

Sydney Garrett stepped inside and commanded everyone's attention. Historically, the military's uniforms, no matter which branch of service, were not all that flattering to a woman's natural curves, and the sterile hairstyles left a lot to be desired. However, Sydney—somehow, some way—strolled into the room and waltzed down the center aisle for a front seat with all the grace and beauty of a runway fashion model.

Jett experienced a stab of disappointment when she walked past and didn't notice him—or pretended not to. One thing *he* noticed was the gold leaf on her uniform.

Captain Sydney Garrett.

She outranked him.

He couldn't help the chuckle that tumbled from his lips, and at the sound of his obvious mirth, a few curious stares were sent his way—including Captain Garrett's.

If she was surprised or shocked to see him, she kept the emotion well contained. And somehow, her continued cool demeanor turned him on.

When his gaze fell on the men surrounding him following Sydney's every move, his face heated and his body coiled tight. The faint voice of reason penetrated his rising tide of jealousy and it took every bit of his military discipline to keep him locked and loaded in his chair.

In the end, he had no choice but to sit and suffer through the men's open gawking toward his—what? The woman wasn't his wife or even girlfriend. Hell, in truth, he hardly knew her. His sudden fierce sense of possession bordered insanity.

At precisely 0830, Major Charles Maxwell moved front and center of the classroom and began his spiel.

"Gentlemen, welcome to Nellis Air Force Base—home of the fighter pilot." Major Maxwell crossed his arms behind his back and paced before the assembled airmen. "Nellis is a member of the air force's Air Combat Command and home of the Air Force Warfare Center. The Warfare Center is the largest and most demanding advance air-combat training in the world. So go ahead. Take a look around."

At his well-rehearsed pause, everyone did as instructed.

Major Maxwell droned on, "You are looking at the best fighter pilots our fine country has to offer. By now you've probably figured out that along with being the best, much more is expected of you. In the next nine weeks, I, along with Lieutenant Colonel Bryant, Major O'Keefe and Major Delsanto will see if you have what it takes to rise to the challenge."

Jett caught the slight nod of Sydney's head and then craned his own to get a good look at her beautifully sculpted face. There was something fascinating about the way she gave the instructor one hundred and ten percent of her attention. There was something sexy about the obvious intelligence radiating from her every feature.

He had to win her. His pride commanded it, his heart…demanded it.

For the rest of the class, Jett hardly paid attention to Major Maxwell's class syllabus while he planned his next tactical move with his beautiful captain.

At 1100 hours, the officers were dismissed for chow, and everyone filed toward the door. Jett suffered through his annoyance at seeing a few of his new colleagues shuffle toward Captain Garrett.

However, she dismissed their advances with her iceberg aloofness and instead headed straight toward him still settled behind his desk.

He gave her a lazy salute and an even lazier smile.

"This is a surprise," she said, ignoring his salute and folding her arms across her chest.

"That is an understatement, Captain." He boldly assessed her figure. "I hardly recognized you."

She smiled. "Has anyone ever told you you're a lousy liar?"

Jett pretended to think the question over. "Hmm. No one comes to mind." He met her gaze head-on. "Has anyone ever told you that you're too serious?"

Her eyebrows rose adorably high. "Just about everyone I've ever met."

"Then it should be your call sign." He eased out of his chair and towered above her. Closing the small distance between them with a half step, he liked the fact she didn't retreat and allowed their bodies to be less than an inch apart. "Unless 'Ball Breaker' isn't being used."

The sweet smell of honeysuckle tickled his nose and became yet one more surprise about this intriguing woman, mainly because he considered the sweetness a contradiction.

"You have to have balls in order for me to break them," she responded with her stone-faced seriousness.

He laughed at the quick retort. "Do you give every man that's interested in you this hard a time?"

Finally, she looked taken aback and Jett drew great pride in scoring a direct hit. "That's it, isn't it? You've been a soldier so long that you've forgotten how to be a woman."

Annoyance flashed across her face. "This conversation is over." She turned on her heel and proceeded to march out of the now-empty classroom.

Jett wasn't about to let her go so fast and strolled behind her and clasped her wrist to restrain her. However, he was not prepared for her to round on him with the fierceness of a caged animal.

"Unhand me, Soldier," she snapped.

He was quickly reminded of the difference in their ranks and his hand fell away as if he were releasing a hot poker.

"Let's get one thing perfectly clear, *Lieutenant.*" Her sable eyes darkened to polished onyx. "While other women may like that cockiness you call charm, I certainly do not. From the moment I met you, you've done nothing but belittle my intelligence, place my life in danger, stand me up and now attempt to manhandle me. I don't know what rock you crawled out of or what village is missing its idiot—"

Jett kissed her. He had to in order to shut her up. And just as he suspected, she melted into him and moaned when he flicked his tongue against hers.

That wasn't to say she wasn't having her own effect on him. His pulse showed no signs of slowing and the heat rushing through his veins refused to cool now he had her in his arms. It was just another confirmation that she was like no woman he'd ever known before.

All sorts of erotic images floated through his head. Pressed against him as she was, he knew her body would be toned and her breasts would be as soft as pillows. And though he had initiated the kiss, he could feel her slow shift to take control.

Surely she would be the same way in bed.

One thing for sure, the longer he kissed her, the harder it became to think. His lungs sang in relief when she broke the kiss, but for a fleeting moment, he was afraid that she was going to start talking again.

Instead, she spun on her heels and marched out of the room.

Jett smiled and shook his head as his gaze swept her backside view through the door's glass window. Still loving what he saw, he released a low whistle to himself. "This is going to be the best nine weeks of my life."

Chapter 8

After the kiss, it took everything Sydney had to walk out of the classroom in a straight line. A thick fog muddled her thoughts, her knees felt paper-thin and the taste of Jett Colton lingered on her lips. What was worse, she could still feel his heavy gaze move up and down her backside. What was he thinking? Did he approve of what he saw?

Now, why in the hell should I care?

She burst through the building's doors and closed her eyes to fill her lungs with Nevada's dry air. The act did nothing to cure her ailments; if anything, it made things worse.

"Nine weeks," she mumbled under her breath.

How in the hell was she going to avoid him for that long?

Once you've seen one chow hall you've seen them all, so Sydney didn't devote much attention to casing the place. She selected her lunch, found an empty, secluded spot and sat down. Making new friends had never been a priority on her list and she saw no reason to change now.

She twirled her fork through her spaghetti bake and told herself to review what was covered in class that morning, but her mind rebelled and *the kiss* replayed in her head—not once, not twice but several times.

After a while, she slowed the picture of Jett's full lips descending toward hers as though she controlled everything by remote control. Each time their lips met, her body experienced the same scorching heat as though it couldn't tell the difference between memory and reality.

"Mind if I join you?"

Sydney's eyes snapped up at the husky female voice and she felt much like a deer caught in headlights. When she reminded herself the woman couldn't see inside her head, and most likely didn't know about her romantic daydreaming, she relaxed. At the same time, the woman seemed to be waiting.

"Excuse me?"

Captain Trenese Post, according to her name tag, had a handsome face split with a wide smile. "Mind if I join you?"

"No, no. Go right ahead." Sydney moved her tray closer and gave her new lunchmate more room.

Captain Post took her seat and then reached her arm across the table. "I'm Trenese, by the way. Friends call me Niecy."

Syd mentally recoiled from the woman's sunny disposition, but shook her hand across the table to accept the greeting. "Sydney."

"Nice to meet you."

Not knowing what else to say, she returned her attention to her half-eaten meal.

"I see you've made another friend today."

Syd's eyebrows dipped together as she brought her head up, however, Niecy wasn't looking at her. Sydney followed the captain's line of vision and was knocked off guard when her gaze crashed into that of Lieutenant Colton. Forcing herself to remain calm, she turned back around.

"Talk about undressing someone with their eyes," Niecy commented. "I'd say he's imagining you naked and draped across his bed." She swung her smiling brown eyes back to Syd. "I guess that makes you the luckiest woman in the room."

Speechless, Sydney took another bite of spaghetti.

Captain Post smirked while she took the first bite of her meal. By the time she swallowed, she seemed confident with herself for having vetted Sydney's character.

"Lieutenant Colton and I were at McDill in

Florida together a few years back. Our next stop after training is Afghanistan."

"Been there. Done that. Good luck."

"Thanks." Niecy took another bite of her food and then continued. "First time I laid eyes on him I thought I'd died and gone to heaven." She chuckled and continued with her story without paying heed to the fact Sydney looked anything but amused. "You won't believe the trail of broken hearts he left back at McDill."

Sydney no longer tasted her meal, but continued to eat.

"I'll let you in on a little secret," Post said. "In the three years I've known Lieutenant Colton, I've never once seen him look at a woman the way he's looking at you."

Despite Sydney's determination to be indifferent, Niecy's compliment caused an embarrassing heat flush to rush up her neck and burn her cheeks. What could she say? What should she say?

"So what are you going to do about it?" Trenese probed, taking another bite of her meal.

For Sydney, opening her mouth was easy; forcing words out of it was another thing entirely. But as she held the woman's gaze, a thought occurred to her. "Did he send you over here?"

Niecy laughed. "Quite the opposite, I assure you. If he knew what I just told you, he'd have my hide."

"So you're a friend of his?"

Niecy fell into a brief silence—the first since she'd taken her seat. "Once."

Sydney's gut twisted with jealousy as she rolled her eyes. This felt very high school. Now that she thought about it, it seemed like the perfect juvenile game Jett would revel in. "Then you won't mind telling *your* friend something for me."

Niecy's smile dimmed.

Sydney cast a glance over her shoulder and, just as she had suspected, Jett's steady gaze remained leveled on her while the men around him chatted away.

"Tell him I find his antics silly, his so-called charm dull and immature and his pretty-boy looks a complete turn-off."

Captain Post stared, blinked and then rocked her head back with a hearty laugh.

Sydney wondered whether she was eating with a mad woman.

"I get it," Niecy declared.

"I'm happy for you." Sydney grabbed her tray and pushed back her chair.

"Wait." Captain Post placed a hand on the corner of Sydney's tray. "You're mad. Don't go."

"I'm not mad," she lied. "I just don't like playing games."

"I swear to you, Lieutenant Colton didn't send me over here. Though right about now he's probably wondering what I've said to set you off."

Sydney studied the stranger's face and questioned her own mental health. Why should she care whether or not the woman spoke the truth?

"Please. I was out of line. I apologize."

Aware that a few unwanted gazes skittered her way, Sydney gave the woman a slow nod, and then pushed her chair back up to the table.

Niecy's smile returned, brighter and wider than before. "Are you really not interested or are you playing hard to get?"

Sydney released a long, frustrated sigh. "Are you really this annoying or are you just pretending?"

That comment successfully shaved a few inches off Captain Post's smile. "Look—"

"No. You look." Sydney leaned forward, determined to end this childishness once and for all. "I'm not interested in anything you have to say concerning Lieutenant Colton. Not now, not ever. And while we're at it, I'm not here to make new friends, either. I have plenty. In the sky, in combat, you'll never have to worry. I have your back. I'll risk my life for you *and* for my country. None of that means we have to be friends. In fact, I'd prefer that we weren't."

The women's gazes locked and held.

"Bullshit," Niecy proclaimed. "You don't have any friends."

Against her will, Sydney's poker face melted. "You got me."

* * *

Curiosity and fear were killing Jett as he watched Captain Post and Captain Garrett whisper and toss narrowed glances in his direction. Before Trenese had joined the equation, he honestly gave himself a fifty-fifty chance of charming his beautiful fighter pilot. Now, his odds lingered somewhere in the realm of a snowball's chance in hell.

Lunch ended all too soon. He watched the women as they gathered their trays and walked together back to class.

What was Post telling her? What *wouldn't* she tell her?

His mind raced over the possibilities—and there were a lot of them.

Jett believed Trenese had seized an opportunity to thwart whatever plans he had for or with Sydney because he had turned down several of Captain Post's advances. "Hell hath no fury like a woman scorned," Jett's older brother, Xavier, had drilled into his head. Why hadn't he listened?

Sarah, Cathy, Nancy and Melanie had all been friends or associates of Trenese, much to his dismay—more so now than ever. Jett could just imagine the horror stories his *former* friend took great delight in rehashing to Sydney.

Jett Colton was a dog, a smooth-talking "playa" who was after one thing. He stopped his wild musing scenario and reflected for a moment. Maybe there was some truth in that description.

A few times that afternoon Jett tried to focus on Major O'Keefe's lecture.

"The mission of the 414th Combat Training Squadron is to conduct air-power training exercises known as Red Flags. A Red Flag is a realistic combat-training exercise involving the U.S. and its allies."

Jett's attention boomeranged back to Sydney. He studied and committed to memory her profile. He rather liked the long, graceful line of her neck, the inviting softness of her skin and the long, lush curl of her eyelashes.

If he had to use one word to describe her beauty, it would be *perfection*. What made Captain Garrett so intriguing was that either she didn't know or didn't care about her effect on the opposite sex.

"Any questions?" Major O'Keefe thundered as his dull green eyes searched the faces of his captive audience.

When no hands shot up, the major nodded his satisfaction. "Good. Then I will see everyone here tomorrow morning at 0700 hours—make sure you remember to bring your flight suits. We're hitting the skies. Dismissed."

Everyone sprang from the chairs and filled the classroom with a low murmur as they filed out of the door. Once again, Jett remained in his seat.

He waited and prayed he'd catch Sydney's eyes,

but, as she gathered her things, Sydney's gaze darted in every direction but his.

Captain Post was another story.

Jett felt her heavy gaze long before he looked at her. When he did, Niecy resembled a cat with canary feathers protruding from her mouth. He narrowed his gaze and gave her the slightest nod, signaling his declaration of war.

Captain Post moved next to Sydney and the women fell into another easy stream of conversation. When they walked past his desk, Jett strained to hear Sydney's words.

"You can have him," Sydney said and marched out the door.

Jett closed his eyes and groaned. This might be the shortest war ever fought.

Chapter 9

"So do you like him?" Steven's question filtered through the phone line.

"Of course not." Sydney's indignant voice bounced off the bathroom tile and boomed back at her. As if chastened, she sank deeper into the lavender-and-honeysuckle-scented bubbles and scrubbed the same clean spot on her knee until it glowed red-raw. "Haven't you've been listening to what I've been telling you? The guy is an arrogant ass."

Steven chuckled. "I like him already."

"Will you get serious?" she snapped. "I have to spend the next nine weeks dodging this jerk. He's lucky I didn't report his manhandling to our C.O."

Steven said nothing as Sydney launched herself onto a new soapbox.

"When women bitch about the military's over-testosteroned jerks it's seen as we can't handle the heat," she ranted. "If I file just *one* complaint it will sink my career, and you know it. Let's not talk about what could have happened if someone walked in when he was kissing me!"

"Wait. He kissed you?"

Sydney cursed under her breath. She hadn't meant to share that tidbit of information.

Amusement crept back into her brother's voice. "Did you kiss him back?"

"No," she stressed and ignored the prick of guilt for lying.

"Uh-huh." Steven's doubt resonated through the line.

"Forget it." She straightened up in the tub and shook her head. "I don't know why I bother talking to you."

"Because you don't have *any* friends." He laughed. "I'm your brother, your best friend and your diary all rolled up into one. Lucky me."

"I'm hanging up," she threatened, but had no intention of doing so.

"Oh, c'mon. Don't be like that," Steven pleaded with a soft laugh. "How do you expect me to act when you tell me this guy kissed you and you didn't punch his lights out à la Bobby Blalock?"

Sydney rolled her eyes at the memory of her senior Academy Ball. "Blalock tried to do more than just kiss me," she reminded Steven.

"Most guys do on prom night, but none of them end up in the emergency room with a broken arm and rib."

A laugh tumbled from her lips. "Okay, maybe I overreacted."

"Ha!" he barked. "*Now* you admit it?"

Her smile widened. To tell the truth she was rather proud of herself for teaching Bobby "Octopus Arms" Blalock that when a woman said no, damn it, she meant no. "I admit nothing." She chuckled.

"Figures." Steven released a long sigh. "So what *are* you going to do about this Jett character? If you're afraid to report—"

"I never used the word *afraid*," she corrected. "I said it would sink my career. There's a difference."

"All right. You want your big brother to fly up there and put this guy in his place?"

"No, I don't need anyone to fight my battles," she sulked and played with what few bubbles remained in the tub. "I just wanted to vent. That's all."

"Venting accomplished, Captain," Steven said gruffly. "Now if you don't mind, it's time for me to hit the sack. I have an early-morning appointment."

"You?" she asked not bothering to mask her astonishment. "Wait. What do you consider early?"

"Noon."

She laughed. "I should have known."

"Don't hate me. I'm not interested in doing more by 9:00 a.m. than most people do all day. I'm quite content to study the backs of my eyelids around that time."

"I just bet you are."

Steven's ability just to go with the flow was one of the things Sydney loved about her brother. Routine, regime and discipline stifled him. He was never meant to work for "the man" as he liked to put it, and he sure wasn't going to join the military. It was strange; Steven, the spitting image of their father, had inherited their mother's free spirit, whereas Sydney, who looked like a younger version of her mother, had inherited her father's personality.

Steven emitted his first yawn of the evening. "So. What you're going to do?"

"Do?"

"About your Romeo."

An instant image of Jett's penetrating golden eyes somehow knocked the chill off the tub's cooling water. "There's only one thing I can do. Stay the hell away from him."

As Major O'Keefe had promised, the students of the 414th met and suited up for their first air combat training. To her surprise, she had been teamed up with the ever-exuberant Captain Post. Sydney swallowed her groan; she and Post were the only women in a class of seventy and she could sense the men in the squadron were already making bets that the "girls" were easy prey.

"This is not a game," Major Maxwell barked. "This is a test," he stressed, marching in front of the group outside the hangar. "Three teams go up— only one team will be declared a winner. The rules? There are no rules—as long as you safely land the plane in one piece."

The men turned to each other for high-fives and Major Maxwell had to shout above the din of hoots and hollers.

"This is a one-time thing. We want to see every-one's natural ability and innate behavior. Remember, this is not a game—nor a time to show off. The purpose of this test is to see how well you engage the enemy *and* how well you get out of a jam."

Sydney thrust her chin up, already feeling the rush of adrenaline and the itch to prove herself in the squad—and, of course, to prove that she was a damn good pilot.

Minutes later three teams were organized and Sydney and Captain Post were strapped into their jets and ready to rock 'n' roll. It was the first time in a long while that she couldn't tell whether the ac-celerated beat of her heart was due to her love of flying or to the fact that she was going against Lieu-tenant Johnson and Lieutenant Colton.

The three teams took off in different directions

to follow their instructors and immediately performed a quick-list of tests. During such exercises,
Syd struggled to keep her ego in check and not to
give in to the temptation of being a show-off. Her
experience in the academy had taught her the hard
lesson of just how much the air force frowned on
such behavior.

When she and Post finished their test they were
directed toward their test fly-zone. During their
short flight to the designated area, Syd had only one
objective: teach Lieutenant Jett Colton a lesson.

Jett glided through the air, feeling very much
like the prince of the skies—ready and determined
to prove just who was the top gun. Almost immediately upon entering the test fly-zone, he and his
wingman, Lieutenant Taylor "Puck" Johnson, were
under attack. From whom, he was unable to ascer-
tain. He just knew he had to shake the flyer before
they were able to get a lock on his plane.

This proved difficult to do when more planes
entered the zone and turned what he perceived to be
a simple cat-and-mouse game into a full-blown attack.

Lieutenant Johnson was the first to go down,
while Jett managed to escape more than one close
call. Twenty minutes later, he had eliminated one
pilot from team C. In no time, team B—Captain
Post and Captain Garrett—had eliminated the last
member from team C, which left two against one.

Jett felt like a mouse in a field of starved cats. However, he remained a slippery and elusive mouse for thirty more minutes before nearly eliminating Captain Post in a perfect execution of a glide-and-roll. He didn't see the trap until it was too late when Sydney, popping up from nowhere, got a lock on him.

"All right, guys," Major Maxwell's voice boomed in their headgear. "Good show. Bring it on in."

Jett didn't answer, but instead released a stream of curses throughout his flight back to Nellis. A long list of what he should've and could've done scrolled through his mind, and his temper was nowhere near cooled by the time he climbed out of his aircraft.

As he returned to the group, he saw Sydney and Niecy receiving a series of high-fives and congratulations. When Sydney turned her broad smile and twinkling eyes toward him, his heart seemed to stop beating in his chest. She looked breathtaking, and he almost felt guilty for hating her guts at that moment—almost.

He didn't want to congratulate the ladies, but he felt the expectation from the rest of the group. Niecy eyed his approach and smugly crossed her arms.

When he stopped before them, he lifted a tight smile and forced his congratulations through clenched teeth. "Nice flying, ladies."

Sydney nodded.

"Wow," Niecy commented. "That looked painful."

Sydney elbowed her new friend.

"That's all you're going to get out of me for a streak of luck."

Sydney's smile vanished. "Luck?"

A few men snickered around them and Sydney's face flushed a darker shade of burgundy. Remarkably, she was just as breathtaking angry as she was smiling. How was that possible? "It's no big deal." Jett shrugged. "We all get lucky from time to time."

"Aw," Sydney drawled sarcastically. "Are your little-man feelings hurt because you were beaten by two girls?"

Jett's spine stiffened.

Another round of snickering ensued as Sydney sensed she'd hit the nail on the head. Her smile returned as she eased up close to him. "If you're going to fly against me, always be prepared to lose."

Jett's eyebrows rose. "Is that right?"

"That's right," she affirmed, her eyes and smile absent of amusement.

"Care to make a little wager on that?" he asked.

"What sort of wager?"

"Next time we go up, if I win, you have to go out with me."

"Should have known." Niecy snorted. "You really do have a one-track mind."

Sydney blinked, thrown for a moment, but looked as though she was really considering his proposal. "And if I win?"

He shrugged at the obvious. "You don't have to go out with me."

"I don't have to do that now."

He smirked. "Okay, then what do you want?"

"Simple."

Something told Jett to worry about the sinister twist to her full lips, but as it was he was having a hard time keeping himself from leaning forward and stealing a kiss.

"If I win," she continued, smiling, "then you have to stand before the class and announce that you're an egotistical, sexist bastard who has now seen the error of your ways."

Niecy let out a small hoot.

It was Jett's turn to look horrified. "A little extreme, don't you think?"

"No more extreme than me actually going out with you," she retorted and mimicked Niecy's pose.

Lord knew how much he wanted to kiss that over-confident smirk off her face. Remembering how she had trembled in his arms yesterday, he was certain her bravado was just a front to cover her attraction to him.

"All right," he said, jutting out his hand. "I accept the terms. You have a deal." To his surprise, she hesitated a moment. Had she hoped he wouldn't accept the wager?

At last, she slipped her hand into his. "Deal."

Chapter 10

For the third day in a row, Jett stood before the class with his jaw clenched tight and his pride a thick mass in the center of his throat while he forced the words out of his mouth. "I'm an egoistical, sexist bastard and I've now seen the error of my ways."

"Louder," Sydney commanded with a wink. "I don't think the fellas in the back can hear you."

Jett tried his best to smite her with an intense look, but his efforts were only rewarded with a wider smile. The same smile he'd *thought* he loved a few days ago.

Sydney and Niecy giggled like teenagers from the front seats.

Though Jett no longer wanted to kiss the smirk from Sydney's lips, he certainly wanted to wrap his large hands around her lovely neck and give it a good throttle. He wasn't the only man who wanted to do so. He'd heard whispers when the men got together. Captain Garrett and Captain Post were bruising their egos and carelessly flaunting their victories with smug smiles and girlish giggles.

Okay, maybe they weren't giggles—but it sure sounded like it to a bunch of annoyed and frustrated men.

"Well, thanks again for that lovely announcement," Major Maxwell said, suppressing his own amusement while Jett took his seat. "Looks like next week, I'll have to separate our dynamic duo Garrett and Post—or at the very least pit them against each other to see who's truly the best."

Sydney and Trenese's smiles disappeared as the women quickly sized each other up.

Jett noted their reaction to Major Maxwell's announcement and felt the first real smile he'd had in days slope his mouth. At this point he didn't care who beat Captain Garrett as long as someone did.

"Before I let you fine officers go for the weekend, I have yet another recommendation I advise you keep at the front of your minds." Major Maxwell's shoulders swelled to the size of mountains, the way they usually did when a "speech" was more in the vein of a lecture.

"For the majority of you who are not from our great city of Las Vegas, I'm sure the vice and the temptation the city offers doesn't come as any great shock. One thing you must *not* believe is that whatever happens in Las Vegas stays in Las Vegas. Whatever misconduct you find yourselves in *will* become a part of your permanent record and will guarantee you a trip out of this squadron." Major Maxwell let his words hang in the air as he took his time to meet a few gazes head-on—Jett's included. "You represent our country whether you're in or out of uniform. Do I make myself clear?"

"Sir, yes, sir."

"Dismissed."

Jett bolted out of his chair. He gave no thought to lingering behind and ogling Serious and her partner. He was over that madness. With the weekend laid out before him, he had every intention of enjoying *some* of Las Vegas's temptations. Surely the city's renowned bevy of beauties knew all the tricks of the trade to get Captain Garrett out his system once and for all.

At least he hoped so.

Sydney watched Jett bolt out of the classroom and wondered about the wave of disappointment she felt. Given the short amount of time she'd known Lieutenant Colton, it didn't make sense that she'd actually miss his attention, his arrogance—or his smile.

"So what do you have planned this weekend?" Niecy asked.

Saved from her own troubled thoughts, Sydney replied with a shrug of her shoulders before she stood up from her chair.

"You *are* planning on hitting the Strip, aren't you?"

Here came the part when her new friend found out how boring and uncool she was. "I don't know. Maybe I'll just make it a Blockbuster night." Sydney headed for the door.

Niecy stayed on her heels. "You're joking, right? Our first weekend in Vegas—?"

"Sorry, but I'm not really the party-girl type."

Sydney had marched out of the classroom and was halfway down the hall before Niecy finally had a comeback.

"Well, you don't have to be a *party* girl just to go out for a few drinks and check out the new models rolling out of the peanut gallery."

"Thanks, but no thanks." Sydney forced a laugh. She didn't drink, couldn't dance and positively didn't know how to interact with the opposite sex—meaning flirting, teasing or talking about meaningless topics until she allowed them to drop trou and they pawed each other until the wee hours of the morning.

"Okay, I'm starting to think your call sign should

be Serious, too. C'mon, let's go out, let our hair down and act like cheap whores."

Sydney tossed a curious glance over her shoulder. "Act?"

Niecy's handsome features darkened while a wicked grin crossed her thick lips.

This time Sydney's laugh was genuine. "No, thank you."

"All right…but I bet you Jett is going to be out on the prowl tonight."

The announcement threw Sydney's confident gait off for a moment, but she recovered quickly and hoped above all things that Niecy hadn't noticed. "I couldn't care less what Lieutenant Colton does or doesn't do with his weekend."

Niecy's hearty laugh drew a fair amount of curious glances in their direction—including Jett's, though he marched several feet ahead of them.

Jett's dark gaze scanned over her body for the briefest of seconds, but it was long enough to short-circuit every system in her body. When his attention turned away, another wave of disappointment nearly wiped her out.

"Couldn't care less, my ass," Niecy snickered as she dogged Sydney's heels toward housing. "One would have to be blind, deaf and struck dumb not to notice the sexual tension flowing between you and Mr. 'They call me Jett because I like anything fast.'"

Sydney laughed again, which only weakened the

effect of her denials. "Lieutenant Colton is an ego-istical, sexist—"

"Bastard. Yeah, yeah, I know. The *whole* class knows." Niecy giggled as they entered their building. "Besides, I'm not suggesting until death do you part—"

"You just want me to get laid."

"No, no."

Sydney rolled her eyes while she slid her key into her lock.

"Okay, well—maybe," Niecy admitted. "But, by all means *not* with Colton. What about Lieutenant Johnson? I think he has the hots for you."

"What?" Sydney asked, surprised.

"C'mon. Don't tell me that you haven't noticed."

"I—I…"

"See, women like you make me sick," Niecy declared with disgust. "Beautiful, low-maintenance women who don't notice all the men panting after them." She crossed her arms. "I practically have to be set on fire to get noticed."

"That's not true." Sydney tapped her on the shoulder. "You're very pretty."

"Yeah, thanks." Niecy shrugged and returned to the subject at hand. "Johnson is the guy for you. He's tall, handsome and he rarely smiles—just like you."

"Very funny."

"Oh, come on. Let's go out. I promise you'll have fun."

* * *

"So what's the real story between you and Serious?" Lieutenant Jim "Weasel" Hawley, another
member of 414th, asked Jett as they cruised toward
the famous Palms Casino.

"What do you mean?"

"Why do you keep letting her humiliate you in
class? You two have a love thang going on or
something?"

Jett rolled his eyes as he shifted in the passenger
seat of Jim's black Explorer.

"Don't get me wrong. I think Serious is hot, too,
but don't you think you might be carrying things a
little too far?"

"Last I checked, I wasn't the only person Captains
Garrett and Post were humiliating in the squadron."

"No, you're just the only one standing in front of
the classroom castrating himself. That shit ain't
cool, man—unless you're laying the pipe down fast
and heavy on the girl."

Jett balled his hand and shot Hawley a warning
glare.

"Hell, if you're not hitting it, then I'm definitely
going to make a move. If you ask me—"

"Which I haven't."

"A good tumble is what the girl needs. Hell, a
few of the guys have a little pool going."

Jett balled his other hand. "What sort of pool?"

Weasel cackled while he kept his eyes on the

road. "You know what kind of pool. Of course, the only question is whether you are doing all this ego-istical-sexist-bastard routine as a way of biting in on our action. You're more than welcome to toss a few dollars into the pool yourself."

The urge to kick Weasel's ass didn't wane when Jett counted to ten or twenty, but somewhere around the number fifty, he realized that he had no real re-lationship with Sydney Garrett and he couldn't order a squadron of gambling bastards to stay away from her—not that any of them stood a better chance of thawing the block of ice around her than he did. Of course, he didn't like the idea of them trying, either.

He exhaled a frustrated breath. All he wanted to do tonight was to forget about the insufferable ace pilot and before he could even execute his plan, he was submerged in thoughts about how to protect her from cads like Weasel.

"So what do you say, Jett? Are you in or out?"

Chapter 11

Nothing in Sydney's well-organized life had ever prepared her for the Palms Casino's nightclub, Rain. Gigantic fireballs lit up an elevated dance floor while hard bodies rocked and gyrated to a thunderous hip-hop beat. At that moment, Sydney couldn't recall how Niecy had talked her into coming to this place.

Nor could she remember how she was talked into wearing one of Niecy's dresses—a short dress. If Niecy hadn't become a fighter pilot she would have made one heck of a used-car dealer.

"Niecy, I don't think this was a good idea," Sydney shouted, tugging on the hem of her skirt, which stopped at midthigh.

"Why?" Niecy bounced to the rhythm. "This place is jumpin' and we look hot."

To support her declaration, two men with overly buffed bodies crowded their space and leered down their plunging necklines.

"Wanna dance?" one with an LL Cool J smile asked, and then slid an arm around Sydney's waist before waiting for an answer.

Sydney pried his arms off. "No."

"Yes," Niecy countered and jabbed Sydney sharply in the side.

"What the—?"

"Dance with the man," Niecy urged with a shove.

Before Sydney could think, her body was rammed against the stranger's. His beautiful smile widened but his overpowering cologne was almost enough to do her in.

"I—I don't dance," she stammered and tried to step back.

His steel grip kept her in place. "You do now." He rocked his hips as he led her to the dance floor.

Sydney remained stiff in his arms while a mild case of panic rose within her. "No. You don't understand," she shouted at the handsome stranger as she tried to pull away. "I don't know *how* to dance."

She hoped the declaration would win her freedom, but the insistent man led her toward the crowded dance floor. Desperate, Sydney dug in her heels and was prepared to clobber the guy if he didn't listen to reason.

"C'mon," he encouraged. "I'll teach you a few moves."

"I—I'm thirsty," she said and immediately sensed her dance partner's disappointment. He covered well and quickly flashed another smile. "Need a few drinks to loosen up, eh?"

They changed directions and headed toward one of the bars. It appeared more crowded than the dance floor.

"What's your poison?" the guy asked.

"A Coke will do."

He stopped in his tracks and turned to face her. "Coke and what?"

She blinked. "Coke and some ice?"

His eyes danced with his bark of laughter. "Just coke and ice? No rum or anything *alcoholic?*"

"Oh." She blinked again. "I don't drink alcohol."

"Uh-huh." He folded his arms and leaned in close in order to be heard over the music. "Is there anything that you *do* do?"

I can knock you on your ass.

"Either I've had too much to drink or my eyes are playing tricks on me," Weasel shouted and pointed across the club.

Jett's gaze followed, but he wasn't sure what he was supposed to see among the sea of people. He opened his mouth to question his colleague when his eyes locked on a stunning beauty in a short, tight minidress. The woman's legs seemed to go on forever. Yet, there was something familiar about the curve of her backside and her graceful posture.

A smile curved his lips while his hands itched to run through her long, wavy hair. If he were a betting man, he'd lay his chips on the woman's thick mane being one hundred percent natural.

"Looks like I've found my lady of the evening." Jett set his glass down and peeled himself away from the small circle of women he and Weasel held court over.

A couple of the women protested while trying to figure out who had caught his attention.

Weasel laughed as he shot out a restraining hand to Jett's shoulder. "Don't tell me you don't recognize her."

Jett frowned and took another look. This time what he saw astonished him. "It can't be."

He blinked, but Sydney "Serious" Garrett's angelic face continued to smile from across the room. He'd always considered her a natural beauty, but he definitely had a soft spot for this pussycat version.

He reached for his drink again.

"I thought you were going over," Weasel chuckled.

Jett shot him an evil glare.

One of the women in their circle brushed her body against Jett and cooed in his ear. "There's nothing over there that you can't get right here."

His gaze swept over the provocative woman, but she no longer looked as alluring as when he'd first offered to buy her a drink. Her makeup was too thick—her eyes too hard. Jett smiled, but his eyes glanced across the room again against his will.

The humiliation he'd endured the last few days still left a bitter taste in his mouth, but he was more than a little disturbed about the attention Sydney drew as time ticked along. In five minutes, she looked as if she was holding her court with fools and jesters trying to get as close as possible.

Finally, he shook his head and then drained the rest of his drink. "I knew she was nothing but a big tease."

"Yeah," Weasel agreed—also ignoring the bevy of beauties surrounding them.

Jett flashed him another narrowed glare.

"What?" Weasel shrugged. "I'm in the pool, too."

The pool. How could he have forgotten about that damn thing?

Jett's arm candy grew impatient. "How about we head out to the dance floor and you can watch me drop it like it's hot?"

It was on the tip of Jett's tongue to refuse the offer when he suddenly came back to his senses. Sydney was not the girl for him. She was the competition. He smiled at the woman on his arm and stood from his chair. "Let's see what you got."

* * *

Sydney wanted to head back to the base. Just as she suspected, she stuck out like a sore thumb and she was growing tired of warding off offers to dance and apparently the only real sin in Las Vegas was *not* drinking alcohol.

"You got a boyfriend?" the latest nameless guy inquired, leaning close—a little too close—into Sydney's personal space. At least he was cute…in a Boris Kodjoe way.

She hitched one shoulder and pretended that she wasn't flattered by all the attention she was getting. In truth, her ego couldn't get much bigger. One thing for sure, it was a stark contrast to her academy days.

However flattered she felt, it vanished when her new hunk gave Bobby "Octopus Arms" Blalock a run for his title. Every time she peeled a hand from her breast, hip and once, her butt, there seemed to be three more strategically placed somewhere else.

After ten minutes of this foolishness, Sydney was at the end of her rope.

"C'mon," the man cooed, clamping a firm hand on her breast again. "Don't you know that whatever happens in Las Vegas stays in Las Vegas?" The jerk had backed her into a corner.

Major Maxwell's warning rang in Sydney's head while she tried, this time unsuccessfully, to remove his hand. "I'm a high-stakes roller. Anything you want I can get. In fact, why don't we go to my suite where we can have some real fun?" the man said.

"I don't think so." She shoved at his chest, but apparently he thought she was playing hard to get.

"C'mon. You didn't come dressed like that just to hold up the wall."

The comment delivered a sharp blow to Sydney's pride. "What's wrong with the way I'm dressed?" The ridiculousness of her question struck her the moment the words were out of her mouth.

He erased what little distance remained between them. Meanwhile, the man's stubborn hand gave a painful squeeze to her breast. "I can't believe a woman as beautiful as you doesn't have an official fan club."

That's it. It's time to take him down.

"She does." A surprising, but unmistakable baritone spoke from behind them. "I'm the president."

Sydney jumped and swiveled around to Jett's handsome features glaring down at the man at her side.

"I think you were just leaving." The muscles flexing in Jett's jaw belied his calm tone.

Sydney's mouth dropped, ready to protest. Who asked for his help? She could take care of herself. To her surprise her nameless suitor seemed unfazed by Jett's macho act and stepped into the line of fire.

"I don't see a ring on her finger."

"That's funny." Jett grabbed the front of the man's shirt and jerked him a full inch off the ground within a blink of an eye. "I see one. Maybe you're not looking hard enough."

Sydney gaped, blinked and stammered before she finally reacted. "Put him down," she insisted and rushed around the startled man. She reached up to break Jett's hold, but it was like trying to break steel.

Her would-be suitor sputtered an awkward laugh. "Hey, man, it's all good." He licked his lips nervously. "I didn't know she was your girl."

"I'm *not* his girl," she snapped at the sputtering fool and then returned her glare back to Jett. "Unhand him."

Jett's lips sloped unevenly. "We're just having a friendly conversation. Isn't that right, buddy?"

The fool just nodded.

"Lieutenant Colton, need I remind you that I'm your superior officer?"

Jett turned his cold gaze in her direction.

Her stomach twisted into knots, but Sydney held her ground and settled her hands on her hips. "Unhand him. That is a direct order."

Jett released the man with a rough shove. "Yes, sir."

Her drunken Casanova hit the floor, butt-first, and then scampered away.

Sydney and Jett hardly noticed as their gazes crashed.

"Is that how you thank someone for rescuing you from as asshole like that?"

"Who said that I needed rescuing? I'm perfectly capable of taking care of myself."

"Yeah, you were right on top of the situation," he said, sneering with sarcasm. His eyes raked her attire. "Maybe you like men groping you in dark corners. Is that it?"

Jett followed her until, once again, she was backed into a corner. The knots in her stomach twisted tighter and she unwittingly lowered her eyes to the inviting shape of his lips. Suddenly, her mouth felt as dry as the Sahara.

What if he kisses me again?

The thought set off a mild panic. "What are you doing?" she asked bluntly and cringed at how badly her voice trembled.

"I'm giving you what you want." Lazily he glided his finger across her bare shoulder. "Attention."

She slapped his hand away. "That's not why I came here."

Unfazed, his hand returned and stroked a trail of fire across her collarbone. "And you didn't wear this fantastic dress that shows off your gorgeous legs as a way to drive every man in here crazy?" He leaned close and inhaled her fragrance.

"I— They are not."

"Oh, but they are."

Another blaze of fire raced up Sydney's leg and she suddenly knew where Jett's other hand had disappeared.

"Mmm. They're so soft and toned." His dark eyes slowly followed the plunge of her neckline. "I imagine other parts of you are the same way."

"Y-you'll never know." She meant to shove him away but only got as far as pressing her hands against his hard chest. After that, the ability to think proved impossible.

His lips sloped. "You're always issuing challenges."

A smile danced in her eyes. "And you're always losing them."

"It's not wise to constantly underestimate me, Captain. Especially when it comes to my getting something I want."

Their eyes locked and it was impossible for Sydney to mistake his meaning. When the seconds stretched into a full minute and she couldn't think of a snappy comeback, she watched with fascinated horror as Jett's mouth descended toward hers.

"Don't," she pleaded.

He stopped with one brow higher than the other. "Is that a direct order, Captain?"

Yes. "No."

Chapter 12

This was a big mistake.

Sydney realized it long before Jett's warm and demanding lips took possession of her own—long before her knees weakened and her heart raced like an Olympic sprinter. As time ticked by, the kiss sweetened and nearly sent her body into a diabetic shock. She moaned despite her attempt to control her rioting emotions, but she was confident the sound was lost in the loud music surrounding them.

However, unlike their first *inappropriate* kiss, Sydney wasn't content to just lie back and enjoy the ride. Her own curiosity and tendency to dominate grew. Soon, she was kissing him with just as much—if not more—passion. When he slid one hand around her waist, she countered by gliding hers up his steely chest.

Jett pressed closer and ignited a blistering fire between them. For once in Sydney's life, she refused to be cowed by it. She *wanted* to be burned—scorched by everything he had to offer.

"What in the hell—?"

Before Sydney had a chance to process the interruption, Jett's large body was jerked back—and whatever spell she'd been ensnared in vanished like a puff of smoke. In its place a familiar wave of embarrassment washed over her.

Niecy, in her annoying splendor, stepped in between the flushed couple with all the fury of an Amazon warrior. "You—" she jabbed her finger in the center of Jett's chest "—stay the hell away from her."

Jett's brows seesawed with amusement. "You've got to be kidding me."

"Does it look like I'm kidding?"

She actually looked murderous.

"You look like you're interfering in something that doesn't concern you." He looked around Niecy's immobile body and pierced Sydney with an annoyed glare. "You want to call off your friend?"

Sydney blinked, unsure why she was so slow to react. "Um, Niecy. It's okay. We were just…"

Niecy crossed her arms while her face twisted with disappointment.

"Everything is fine," Sydney finally settled on saying.

Niecy shook her head and clamped a hand on Sydney's arm and pulled her aside.

"Hey," Jett called.

"Hold your britches," Niecy snapped, but continued to lead Sydney to a secluded corner. "What gives? I thought you weren't interested in that fast-talking Casanova?"

"I'm not," Sydney lied and pulled her arm free.

"Do I look like I was born yesterday? Do I need to remind you of how many women—friends of mine—he's blown off after he—?"

"No." Sydney moaned and pinched the bridge of her nose as if the act would stop reason and caution from flowing back into her brain. So what if he'd had a lot of women? So what if he'd left a trail of broken hearts across the country? She wasn't like other women. She knew how to be careful and protect herself. Hell, she'd done it all her life.

"I'm just…having some fun." She dropped her hands and shrugged. "Isn't that what you said I should do? There's no crime in that and I'm a big girl."

Niecy rolled her eyes and shook her head. "I can't tell you how many times I've heard that, too."

Sydney felt her own annoyance mount. "What's the *real* deal with you?" she asked, crossing her arms. "What's with the personal interest? Are you pissed that Jett is interested in me or the fact that he has *never* been interested in you?"

When Niecy jerked back with wide, angry eyes, Sydney had her answer.

"Fine," Niecy hissed. "You're on your own. When you're left crying in your pillow, remember this moment."

Sydney didn't get a chance to rebut the declaration before her friend—probably now her ex-friend—turned and disappeared into a sea of partygoers.

"Can't say that I'm sorry to see her gone," Jett deadpanned when he reclaimed his position next to Sydney. "Now, where were we before we were so rudely interrupted?" He slid his hand back around her waist.

Sydney stepped out of his grasp in order to maintain a clear head. "Don't. I'm not having fun anymore."

He ignored her aversion and cornered his prey. "That's because we still have our clothes on. What do you say we get a suite and see how fast I can sink my battleship?"

Sydney's face twisted in horror. "I keep forgetting how cheesy your pick-up lines are."

"Maybe," he whispered and stole a quick kiss just below her earlobe, and then leveled his golden gaze on her. "But I'm incredibly cute."

"That settles it." She ignored the electricity of his touch and pushed him away. "I'm heading back to the base." She took one step, but Jett quickly drew her back.

"All right. Since getting butt-naked is out of the question…Captain. How do *you* propose we spend our first weekend in Sin City?"

"Apart." She peeled his hands away. "We're like oil and water—we don't mix."

"Aw, c'mon. That's the alcohol talking. We get along fine."

"I don't drink." She crossed her arms. "And where was all this camaraderie when I was kicking your ass in combat training?"

The muscles twitched along Jett's jaw, signaling she'd, once again, struck a nerve. "You've been lucky," he said.

"Trust me. It doesn't take a whole lot to beat that hotdogging you call flying."

"Hotdogging?" His eyes narrowed and then raked over her. "You know, you're right. This is a mistake—Captain."

"Glad you agree." She turned.

"I should have known you couldn't stop pretending to be a man long enough to have a good time. Maybe it was the dress that fooled me."

Sydney whipped around. "What did you say?"

Jett ignored her outrage and signaled a waitress. "Whiskey straight up."

Sydney crowded his personal space and took a

page out of Niecy's book to jab a finger in the center of his chest. "I asked you a question."

Jett's eyes glowed like molten gold. "You heard me. What's the matter—daddy not love you enough?"

The slap stung and surprised them both.

"My father was more of a man than you'll ever be—you self-righteous son of a bitch! If your pride is so easily bruised because you're a lousy pilot, then maybe you should look into another career. One where lives don't depend on you doing your job."

Jett's anger boiled and what he longed to do more than anything was to wrap his hands around her beautiful neck. But at the end of her holier-than-thou speech his heart quickened at the sudden gloss of tears in her eyes.

She bolted from him and this time he wasn't quick enough to stop her.

"Your whiskey, sir." The waitress returned with a bright smile.

He grabbed the drink and tossed some bills onto the tray before he drained the glass in one quick gulp. The liquor's burn gave him the jolt he needed before diving into the pulsing crowd. The experience felt like looking for a needle in a haystack.

The minutes stretched and his alcoholic buzz vanished while he combated a rising wave of panic. What on earth had possessed him to say that to her? Why was he so hell-bent on conquering her iron will?

Truth be told, he wanted more than to conquer—

he wanted to dominate. Every night in the past week he'd done nothing more than dream of how he was going to accomplish his goal—and every morning, *she* out-flew, out-maneuvered—out-everythinged him while reducing his ego to the size of a peanut.

Jett stopped his search in the middle of the dance floor. What was the point? What could he possibly say about his thoughtless remarks?

A few women swiveled and eased up on him, but he wasn't in the mood to dance or party anymore. He scanned the club again. This time he looked for Weasel. When this proved impossible, too, he headed for the door.

During the long trek out of the club, Jett obsessed over his harsh words to Sydney. He was the last one who should talk about someone's father given the fact his couldn't stand his guts.

My father was more of a man than you'll ever be.

Was. Jett cursed under his breath and blocked out the flash of pain he'd witnessed in her eyes. He really did need to learn to think before he spoke.

Finally, he exited the club and drew in a deep breath. However, the hardest thing to do in Las Vegas is find solitude. From the party crowd to the gambler's den, Jett searched for a place where he could be alone with his thoughts.

"You look like someone has kicked your puppy."

Jett glanced up, momentarily surprised to find his feet had led him to a bar in the center of the casino.

That surprise was eclipsed when he recognized Niecy nursing a drink and plopping quarters into a counter video poker machine.

"What—are you stalking me or something?"

"I was here first."

"A small technicality." He shrugged and then slid onto the stool next to her. "Where's your friend?"

"How should I know?" Niecy folded her arms. "I left her with you."

Jett exhaled and planted his elbows on the bar. "Well, she's no longer with me." He signaled the bartender and ordered, "Whiskey straight up."

"What did you do?"

He resented the question and clamped his jaw tight.

"Well?" she asked, ignoring his body language.

"What makes you think *I* did something?"

Niecy's thin, arched brows leaped high. "Is that a real question?"

His drink arrived and Jett tossed the liquor down as if it were water.

"That bad, huh?"

"That bad," he mumbled.

Neither spoke, but the casino's loud hum of laughter, slot machines and exuberant gamblers filled the space between them.

"You keep looking like that and I'm going to actually think you care about Serious."

Jett grunted. Though he was in no mood for Niecy's baiting, he couldn't bring himself to leave her company. He mulled that over for a moment. It certainly had to be more evidence of his plummeting sanity.

"Well, she's different. I'll give her that," Niecy said, chucking more money into the machine. "Especially if she's showing signs of immunity to your...charm."

"Bartender, I'll have another," Jett called out.

"You got it," said the young man who held a startling resemblance to Tobey McGuire.

"All right, stop it." Niecy abandoned her game and turned her full attention to Jett. "You keep sulking and I'm actually going to start feeling sorry for you."

"Keep your pity." He straightened in his chair when his drink arrived. His callous words to Sydney looped in his head while his father's bloated face surfaced in his mind.

Worthless bastard. You're never going to amount to anything.

Jett closed his eyes, hating how his father's words always reduced him to feeling like a vulnerable six-year-old. He'd spent most of his life trying to prove his father wrong, trying to win his love.

The love he gave so freely to his older son, Xavier.

Xavier had never had to deal with their father's physical or verbal abuse. Good old dad reserved all that just for little James. However, both heard his constant proclamation about their mother being a whore. That word was a source of confusion until

Jett turned ten and realized that he didn't look like anyone in the family. Eyes the color of wheat had a way of sticking out among a family tree of black onyx, and when both sides of the family showcased skin the color of dark chocolate, one had to wonder how Jett had inherited his light coloring.

Plain and simple, Gerald Colton had no room in his heart to love a son who wasn't his.

Love. He chuckled under his breath. What did he know about the elusive emotion? Hell, it was just a word as far as he was concerned. Heaven knows, he'd searched for it in buxom breasts, hourglass curves and soft, plump lips. However, no woman had ever elicited an emotion that had lasted outside of the bedroom.

"So much for love," he mumbled.

Niecy frowned. "You love her?" she asked, misunderstanding him.

"No." Jett laughed. "I'm just intrigued by her." *And her passionate love for her dead father.* He finally stood up and tossed money onto the counter. "Last time I checked that wasn't a crime."

Niecy studied him. "Do you need a ride back to the base?"

"I'll catch a cab."

"It will cost you a fortune."

"Hey, Jett. There you are." Weasel hooked his arm around Jett's neck as he approached from behind. "Man, I found us a couple of honeys that don't know the meaning of the word *no,* if you catch my drift." He barked out a laugh.

"How charming." Niecy snorted.

"Ah, Captain Post." Weasel wheeled around to face her with a mock salute. "I didn't see you sitting there."

Her eyes narrowed on him. "By all means, pretend that I'm not."

"As you wish, Captain." He spun back toward Jett and nearly lost his balance in the process. "So, what do you say, Jett? Care to join us—or are you still trying to win that pool? I saw you with—"

"I'm not trying to do anything." Jett cast a nervous glance over at Post.

"What pool?" she asked. Her eyes filled with a renewed suspicion.

"Nothing." Jett shook his head and tried to tug Weasel away from the bar. "He's obviously had too much to drink."

"Oh, I get it," Weasel slurred with a dramatic wink. "Mum's the word."

Jett clamped a hand over his friend's mouth. "We'll catch you later." He turned and literally dragged Weasel away.

Niecy watched the circus act of Weasel, Jett and two scantily clad women melt back into the casino crowd. "Those two are up to something," she muttered.

Hostile territory…

Chapter 13

Tuesday, July 4, 2006: 1600 hours. Osan Air Base

The 21st Special Operation Squadron—the newly reestablished Black Knights—were locked and loaded for their search-and-rescue mission, Jett included. Despite not having a formal introduction to his new C.O., he'd had no problem getting on active duty, since the base had grabbed every able body they could find.

Osan was no longer operating in the dark. All systems were up and running—though no concrete explanation had been found as to what had caused the four-hour blackout. This was an unacceptable answer from the brigadier general all the way up to the president of the United States.

North Korea's chief of state, Kim Jong-il, filled the airwaves with threats of a nuclear attack in response to their country's energy crisis. All talks with South Korea, Japan and the United States were cut off.

While the world held its breath during the standoff, Jett's heart and soul obsessed over one thing—one person.

She's not dead. She can't be dead. I would feel it, wouldn't I?

He wasn't sure anymore. Time played cruel tricks. In the three years since Sydney had walked out of his life, why hadn't he gone after her? Lord knows he wanted, needed and longed for her. Hell, he still remembered vividly the taste and feel of her as if she'd put a curse on him.

For three years he'd tried to replace her in his heart, but her lips had soured the taste of other women. His body was enslaved, never able to experience the rapture her curves and feminine softness provided with any other woman. Though their paths had failed to cross again, he'd fooled himself into believing that someday they would, but now...

"Charlie Two-Seven, you are cleared for takeoff."

The sharp voice from traffic control crackled inside the headset and wrenched Jett back to grim reality.

"Roger that." Jett turned up his engine to full

power, but then his hand felt cold and sweaty as he wrapped it around the throttle. He drew a deep breath, steadied his racing heart and forced himself to remain in the present. He needed to be at the top of his game when flying into enemy territory. He had to be better than he had ever been if he was going to survive and rescue the woman he should never have let go.

Every inch of Sydney's body hurt—and *not* in a good way. If it weren't for the questionable species slithering in the vicinity of her open thighs she would have been content to lie still and bake in the sun for eternity. However, rectifying the situation meant moving and moving meant more pain.

Who, what, why and where she was raced like a train through her mind, but no ready answer was forthcoming. She just wanted and needed to survive the pain. Whatever was taking the liberty of gliding all over her body now had a firm hold of her leg and was squeezing painfully hard. So much so that she finally managed the impossible task of opening her eyes. A carpet of rich green stretched out before her, which only confused her more.

The pressure on her leg intensified and she tried to flail her hands—up, down. Was she upside down? Wait. That didn't make sense. *Pain. Stop the pain.*

She jammed her hand into her vest, fumbled for a moment, but then finally wrapped her hand around the semiautomatic Beretta. The pain had robbed her of logic. It must have. It was the only explanation for why she would purposely shoot blindly toward her own leg.

Instantly her slippery assailant released its hold on her—as did gravity—and she found herself plunging head-first toward the ground. Shortly before she hit the bottom, it occurred to her that she was sliding down a tree—a massive tree.

The inevitable crash came, flipping her body forward, where she landed unceremoniously against sharp rocks embedded in the earth. Sydney lingered at the edge of darkness for a moment, but then oxygen seeped back into her lungs.

Somehow, she managed to roll herself over and open her eyes once again. This time, she stared at nothing but blue sky. The beauty of it didn't escape her. In fact, it gave her a sudden strength while it cleared the clouds from her mind.

"My name is…" She coughed, gasped and then licked her lips as a way to stall for answers. "I'm Major Sydney Garrett of the U.S Air Force." A proud smile cracked her dry lips as she then rambled off her serial number. Then she tried to answer the question of why she was lying on the ground, but the last thing she remembered was coasting on a routine sortie near the DMZ.

She searched her memory for what seemed like eternity but kept hitting a brick wall. With prayer and flagging strength, Sydney pulled herself up into a sitting position. Half of a snake's corpse still clung to her left leg, while its blood—or hers—was splattered across her ripped and singed G-suit.

Singed—fire.

A brief image of a jet's cockpit ablaze flashed through her mind. Her hand trembled as she lifted it and gently pressed her fingers against her face. A surge of renewed pain ripped through Sydney and she quickly removed her hand.

Just like that she remembered everything. She closed her eyes and forbade her burning tears to fall. *Pull yourself together. Soldiers don't cry.*

She repeated her lifelong mantra until courage trickled back into her veins. True, every inch of her body throbbed with pain, but everything seemed to be in working condition. That is until she tried to stand up.

Her left ankle was shattered. Every time she moved it, the pain overwhelmed her. Sydney took in her surroundings, this time straining her ears for any sound.

Silence greeted and terrified her.

As best as she could tell, she was in the woods or a forest. At least that could help her to hide from the enemy. Of course, it would also make it harder for a search-and-rescue team.

After what seemed like hours, Sydney managed to drag herself behind a thicket of trees and hunker down. She unclipped the kit attached to her hips and then removed the radio from her survival vest. She switched on the channel and made a desperate attempt to reach her wingman.

"Puck, this is Serious. Come in." She kept to their call signs as a way to camouflage her identity in case enemy forces were listening.

No response.

She tried again, but the radio remained dead in her hand.

Emotionally, she stood at a crossroads. One path would lead her to despair and depression. The other meant she would have to fight like hell to survive. She had to survive. There was something that she still had to do. There was something that she still had to say—to confess.

Again, a pair of twinkling gold eyes flashed in her memory, along with a brilliant smile that warmed her like the sun.

I should have told him I loved him when I had the chance.

Despite her best efforts, tears seeped from her eyes. But her survivor instincts and courage were rising by leaps and bounds. *I will get another chance.*

Sydney lifted the radio to her mouth. "Puck, this is Serious. Do you read me? Come in."

The birthday gift…

Chapter 14

Jett and Sydney went out of their way to ignore each other. But the competition between them remained fierce—in and out of the sky. Their 5:30 a.m. physical training class had them competing in everything from five-mile runs to scaling walls in Olympic time.

The runs nearly always ended in a tie but Jett practically gloated when he beat her over the wall. Yet, once they were in the sky, no one beat Sydney Garrett.

"All right, everyone, listen up," Major Maxwell commanded and then paced before the hangar.

"Today we're going to be working in the simulator where each of you will be tested against surface-to-air missile launches."

Sydney's stomach lurched, but she made certain she kept her anxiety hidden.

"Captain Garrett. You're up first."

"Yes, Major." She saluted and stepped out of ranks to follow her instructors to the simulator. Gearing up remained the same as if she were climbing into a F-16. Everything was replicated to give the exact feel of takeoff and flying.

When her threat-warning system lit up, Sydney's hands were suddenly sweaty and her stomach had transformed into a jumble of nerves. "Missiles in the air," she informed tower control as protocol demanded. Next she rattled off her coordinates.

With an arsenal of tricks up her sleeves, Sydney remained confident that she could outmaneuver the attack. A scant minute later that confidence had waned. No matter what she did, the missile remained locked onto her.

Think, Syd. Think.

For the first time, she drew a blank and when she tried to pull a desperate hotdog attempt, the plane's throttle became uncontrollable.

She tried to read her center console, but everything was shaking uncontrollably. Then she felt rather than read when her engine shut down. The next second, she was spinning out of control.

Then everything stopped.

"All right, Captain Garrett. Climb on out. You're dead."

The declaration crushed her, but she said nothing as she unhooked everything and climbed out. When she descended the metal steps from the simulator, a wall of stunned faces greeted her.

"All right. Captain Post, you're up."

"Yes, Major." Niecy saluted and stepped out of ranks.

Sydney returned to the line, walking on numb and shaky legs. What in the hell just happened?

However, Captain Post, as well as the majority of the squadron, met the same fate as Sydney. Then it was Jett's turn.

"Lieutenant Colton. You're up next."

Lieutenant Johnson moved next to Sydney. "Don't beat yourself up. That was a devil test."

Sydney glanced up and smiled into Johnson's kind eyes. "Thanks. I needed to hear that."

Outside the simulator, the rest of the squadron could see the same simulation as the pilot on a wall screen. Sydney, however, was still reviewing in her mind what she'd done wrong when she caught a few whispered questions buzzing around her.

"What is he doing?" Lieutenant Johnson asked.

Sydney glanced up at the screen and saw Jett in a near nosedive toward the missile. Words eluded her as she watched the scene unfold. Her breath even hitched as though Jett had placed himself in real danger.

Then, when a collision was all but guaranteed, Jett performed a perfect glide-and-roll in the opposite direction. The hangar erupted in cheers while Sydney found herself thoroughly impressed.

When Jett emerged from the simulator he received another around of cheers and applause. For the first time in two weeks, Jett's and Sydney's eyes met and held. Finally, she gave him a small smile and a slight nod of congratulations.

"Steven, what do you mean you're not coming? It's my birthday." Sydney moaned into her cell phone as she collapsed onto her rock-hard bed. "I was looking forward to seeing you."

"I was, too, Syd. But Corrine's parents are flying in this weekend. Her father already doesn't like me so I have to be on my best behavior."

"What—are you going to pop the question or something?"

Steven didn't respond.

Sydney's eyes widened with shock and her grip tightened on the phone. "Are you kidding me?"

"I bought the ring yesterday."

"And you didn't tell me?" She bounced up off the bed, wishing he were there for her to hug. "I can't believe it. *You* are getting married!"

"Well, she hasn't said yes yet."

"She will if she has any sense." Sydney spun around in a small celebration. "Gosh, I wish I was there."

"Does this mean that you forgive me for not flying to Vegas for your birthday?"

"Of course. I'll be twenty-eight all year long. It just means that you'll have to buy me a bigger present."

"Deal." Her brother laughed and then quickly sang "Happy Birthday" before ending their call.

Sydney, of course, called her mother and shared the news. After a few excited screams, her mother inquired about her training.

"Your father would've been so proud of you," her mother cooed.

The words comforted Sydney.

"Did you get the present I sent you?"

"Yes. Thanks for the homemade cookies. I've eaten at least a dozen of them."

"Well, make sure that you share them with your friends."

Sydney nodded, though she wanted to laugh. *What friends?* "I will, Momma. In fact, I'd better go. I'm going out with a few of them tonight," she lied.

"That's nice, dear. You have fun."

Sydney ended the call and then wallowed in guilt, even though, in this case, it was better to lie than to let her mother fret about her daughter's nonexistent social life. Tossing her cell phone onto the bed, Sydney glanced around the tiny room in despair.

"Now what?" She thought for a moment and then answered herself. "Well, you can either sit here and sing 'Happy Birthday' to yourself *or* you can go down to the Strip and have your own celebration."

Frankly, singing to herself had more appeal than hanging out with a bunch of strangers.

A knock sounded at the door.

Sydney glanced over and drew a blank as to who it could be. "Who is it?"

"You'll never believe it in a million years."

Her hand froze on the doorknob. "Lieutenant Colton?"

"The one and only."

Sydney's hand flew to her hair, which was a tumbled mess about her shoulders. "Err…uh, just a minute." She pivoted and darted to the bathroom where she quickly ran a brush through her hair. While she was at it, she dug through her makeup bag for her lipgloss so she would have some kind of color on her face.

"Look, I know that you don't want to let me in," Jett shouted through the door.

"No, no. It's not that." She ran from the bathroom and tripped over her bag she'd left by one of the chairs. She hit the floor with a loud "Ooof!"

"Hey, are you all right in there?" Jett asked.

"Fine. I'm fine. I'm coming." Sydney peeled herself off the floor and finished her dash to the door—unaware that her fall had unraveled her violent brush strokes.

When the door finally swung open, Jett jumped back in astonishment. Sydney, usually a very composed individual, looked damn near erotic with her hair tousled about her head.

"Did I interrupt something?" he inquired as he stole a peek into the room over the top of her head. "Is this a bad time?"

"No, no. I was just, uh, chillin' out."

Jett frowned. Street slang sounded as natural from Sydney as it would from Queen Elizabeth. "Just chillin', huh?"

"Yeah." She smiled, but had difficulty maintaining eye contact.

A long silence elapsed while Jett struggled to remember his rehearsed speech. "Look, I know you're probably wondering why I stopped by."

"Probably to rub in my face how I blew today's test." She crossed her arms. "It being your first chance to gloat and all." Finally, their eyes met.

"No." The fact that she was purposely trying to start a fight wrangled a smile from Jett. "Actually, I came to call a truce."

"A truce?" Doubt edged lines into her forehead.

"Yeah." This time he dropped his gaze to study the blue carpet. "And I also wanted to apologize—for what I said about your father. I crossed the line."

That unnerving silence returned. When he looked up, it was to see her eyes glossed with tears.

"You're the best pilot in the squadron. It has nothing to do with your sex. You're just damn good."

Sydney's cheeks darkened as though he was flirting with her.

"And I'm sure that your father was a fine man."

She lifted her chin. "Not only that, he was a great pilot."

In that moment, so much of the mystery that surrounded Captain Sydney Garrett was solved.

"So." Jett clasped his hands behind his back. "What are you doing this Friday evening?"

"I—I, um."

She glanced around as if looking for something to rescue her from this moment. Jett wasn't going to let her off so easily. "Because if you're not doing anything, I was sort of hoping that I could cash in that rain check I have from our first date."

"I didn't give you a rain check. You stood me up."

"A technicality." Jett propped up his arm against the door frame. "But it does appear that we're both free tonight." He was practically willing her in his head to say yes, and promising himself that this time he was going to do everything right.

She glanced back into her room and again he wondered if someone else was in there—someone like Johnson. "I'm not dressed," she said.

His gaze raked over her clothes.

"I mean—I'm not dressed to go out."

Sydney smiled and made his night. "How about I come back and pick you up in about an hour?"

"Are you going to show up this time?"

"Wild horses couldn't keep me away."

Her sexy smile slid wider. "All right. It's a date."

"Good." He straightened and gave her a wink. "I'll see you in about an hour."

Sydney closed the door with a soft click and then leaned against it while she sang, "Happy birthday to me...."

Chapter 15

Sydney rushed to her closet and took out the beautiful red dress her mother had sent for her birthday. Her eyes roamed the soft material while she imaged Jett's reaction when he saw her in it. After she whispered a thank-you to her mother, she hurried to the bathroom to get ready.

During the whole time she got dressed, she tried her best to ignore the voice in her head, warning her to proceed with caution. After all, Jett had let her down a few times already.

"I'm just going out to have a little fun because it's my birthday," she told her reflection in the bathroom mirror. Didn't she deserve a night out on the town?

But what if he kisses you again?

She stopped in the middle of brushing her teeth and gave the question considerable thought. Her body warmed as she thought about the last time he'd kissed her. She remembered how all her thoughts had turned fuzzy, and how she'd melted in his arms.

She hoped he would kiss her again.

Sydney smiled at the delicious thought and then sped through the rest of her ablutions. Makeup on, hair curled and dress on, she was finally ready to knock Jett's socks off.

Exactly one hour after he'd left, there was a knock on the door. At the sound, Sydney's heart raced as if she were preparing for takeoff. In a strange way, maybe that was exactly what she was doing.

When she opened the door, Jett wasn't the only one to gasp in surprise.

"You look—" Jett's beautiful golden eyes took their time as they roamed over her "—ravishing."

Her entire body warmed at his approval. A part of her wondered why she felt and behaved like a lovestruck teenager, but hadn't he always had that effect on her, cheesy lines and all?

"Shall we?" He offered her his arm.

"Just a second." She turned back into the apartment and located her purse. When she returned to the door, she slid her arm through his. "May I ask where we're going?"

Jett shook his head and winked. "It's a surprise."

Sydney smiled as she allowed him to lead her through the building.

It was Friday night and most of the squadron had taken off for the weekend. But there were still a few who performed double takes and elbowed each other when they saw them together.

"Looks like you have a few admirers," Jett whispered to her.

She doubted that. They were probably just stunned to see her in a dress. Jett continued the role of gentleman when they reached the car and he opened her door. "You look like Jett Colton, but you're certainly not acting like him."

He smiled and lightly tipped her chin up so she could meet his eyes. "This is a truce, remember?" He leaned down and brushed a kiss against her lips.

The combination of the night's warm breeze and his pillow-soft lips elicited a moan from her. When she realized what she'd done, another flush of embarrassment burned her cheeks. "A truce, then," she agreed.

Jett waited until she slid into her seat before he closed the door and walked around to the driver's side. Starting up the car, he tossed another wink in her direction and pulled out of the lot.

"So." Jett turned off the radio. "How much flack do you think we're going to get when word gets out we went on a date?"

"A lot," she answered truthfully. "Of course,

most will think you're trying to woo me so I will go a little easier on you the next time I'm up against you." Though it was a statement, Sydney lifted a single brow as if posing a question.

"Damn." Jett stretched in his seat. "Why didn't I think of that?"

She smiled, but wasn't sure whether her curiosity was sated.

"Of course," he continued. "They're probably thinking you simply couldn't resist my charms any longer and lured me away with that sexy dress so you can have your way with me."

She nearly choked on her laughter.

"Hey. It's not *that* funny."

"Oh, yes, it is."

He glanced over at her with a sly smirk. "Then why did you agree to go out with me?"

She thought a moment and weighed whether to tell him the truth. "It's my birthday," she admitted.

He laughed at the notion. "Yeah, right."

"I'm serious." She crossed her arms. "My brother canceled on me at the last moment. Then you showed up and I still wanted to celebrate so I figured that you would do in pinch."

"Ouch. You really know how hurt a brother."

She shrugged. "Well, I guess you still owed me a date."

"Ah, so I did have a rain check? You know, you could have called and told me."

"Just like you could have called while I was still waiting in that restaurant for hours like a fool and told me that you couldn't make it?"

Jett winced. "Sorry. I—I got…sidetracked."

"What was her name?"

He laughed at that, but then realized that it was probably a natural conclusion. "It wasn't a woman."

"Right." Doubt dripped from Sydney's voice as she turned and stared out of the window.

"I was in Atlanta in July visiting my father. When I got to his house—after meeting you—I discovered that he was missing."

His admission got her attention.

"The whole house was ransacked so I started asking the neighbors questions and then friends, the police and then finally strangers. I was worried sick and didn't find him until something like 2:00 a.m."

"Where was he?" she asked in concern.

"He was passed out drunk in the alley of some hole-in-the-wall bar." Jett drew in a deep breath as his hands tightened on the steering wheel.

Sydney watched the tension tighten his jaw. At the same time her heart went out to him. Suddenly, he wasn't the same man she'd known. The one sitting beside her now radiated a different kind of strength—and sadness.

"I'm sorry. I had no idea," she said in a whisper.

Jett smiled, but it looked more like a caricature of a smile. "How could you have known?"

"I could have called and found out why you didn't show up." She remembered her anger that night—remembered all the names she had called him. Now, she felt guilty that she'd never given the man the benefit of the doubt.

She reached over and gave a light squeeze to his arm. "Your father is lucky to have a son like you."

"Yeah, right."

"Oh." Her hand fell away. "You two aren't close?"

Jett broke his silence with a harsh laugh. "Hardly. The man can't stand me."

His anguish caused another pinch to her heart.

The car fell silent again and after brief while, Jett snapped out of his reverie. "Okay, enough of that. I'm ruining your birthday. Since I know that a woman never tells her age—"

"Twenty-eight," Sydney said, perking up. She welcomed the change in topic. Not because it made her uncomfortable, but because of the effect it had on Jett.

"Ah, you're younger *and* you outrank me. Will the surprises never end?"

"How old are you?"

He smiled. "Take a guess."

She studied him and hazarded a guess. "Thirty-five?"

"What?" He exited the highway and then took a look at himself in the rearview mirror. "I look thirty-five already?"

"No, no. Well…yes." She winced. "Aren't you?"

"Thirty."

He pretended that his feelings were hurt, but Sydney caught the way his lips fluttered upward.

"Sorry." She played along. "Maybe you should look into getting a face-lift or something. You know, they say the younger you start the better the results when you're over the hill."

"You're a regular comedian, huh?"

Sydney laughed and enjoyed their light banter. When they arrived at the Bellagio, Sydney worried that he was taking her to another outrageous dance club. Her fears subsided when they arrived, instead, at the Picasso restaurant.

The place was a French-Mediterranean dream. Sydney thought of her mother as they were ushered past the large spray of flowers, the paintings and the sculptures. It was as if she'd been dropped in the middle of a fairy tale.

"This place is gorgeous," she whispered as Jett held out a chair at the table in a small, intimate nook.

"The food here is wonderful," he informed her.

"You've been here before?"

"A few years ago." He shrugged. "When I was stationed in California, Las Vegas became like a second home to me and some of my buddies."

Sydney couldn't picture the Picasso being just a hangout for the guys and jealously wondered if he'd brought another woman here.

The waiter took their appetizer orders and brought out fresh bread. The conversation dwindled, but it was no longer the sort of awkward silence they'd experienced in the car. It was more comfortable and allowed Sydney to soak in the atmosphere.

"Do you like champagne?" Jett asked, picking up the wine menu.

"I don't drink," she said.

"Not even on your birthday?"

"Well…" She teetered on her decision.

"The '88 Salon," Jett ordered and snapped the menu closed. "You can't have a celebration without wine."

He tossed her another wink and she found herself nodding in agreement.

"So." Jett leaned closer. "Tell me a little about yourself—outside of the military."

She laughed awkwardly, thinking that most of her identity was wrapped up in her career. It was, as her brother always reminded her, what she lived and breathed for. "Well, I was born in Atlanta, Georgia, but my family moved around a lot because of my father's military career. I have an older brother, Steven. I developed my love of flying from my father—and my grandfather. I'm a World War Two enthusiast, as are most fighter pilots. I graduated from the Air Force Academy in Colorado at the top of my class—"

"Now why doesn't that surprise me?"

"Truce, remember?"

"Sorry. Please continue."

"Actually, that's about it," she concluded as their wine arrived at the table.

The waiter showed Jett the label.

Jett nodded and returned his attention to Sydney. "What do you mean that's it?"

"I mean that after the academy I went to flight school and then I was stationed at Randolph Air Force Base in Texas and Moody in Georgia. A year later 9/11 happened and I was deployed to Afghanistan. My tour ended, I returned to Moody and then I was sent here."

"You've seen action?"

"Who hasn't?"

He nodded in agreement. "Interesting, but you left a lot of stuff out, didn't you?"

"What do you mean?"

The waiter poured her a glass of champagne.

Jett rested his chin atop his steepled hands. "I mean, your dating experience. Your first love, your first kiss, and…so on."

Sydney reached for her glass the moment it was set on the table and downed more than half its contents in one gulp.

Jett's amusement lined every inch of his face. "Careful. You probably have a low tolerance for alcohol."

After experiencing a sudden rush of blood to her head, she had to agree.

"Well?" he asked. "Tell me about your first love."

She hedged a little longer, weighing whether she wanted to travel down the lonely, desperate road that was her love life. "Romeo Tillman."

"Romeo? Really?" He chuckled with a measure of disbelief.

"The name made him all the more perfect." Sydney teased him with a smile.

"Good point," he conceded. "Continue."

Drawing a deep breath, she leaned back in her chair while she strolled down memory lane. "Romeo, oh, Romeo." She sighed. "How much thou broke my heart."

Jett sobered at her sad declaration.

"I was fourteen. I was a sophomore—and worse, a late bloomer, and he was a senior. Aw, man. He was like a God. All the girls were crazy about him. And he certainly had a reputation for being the best...*kisser* on campus."

Jett's brows lifted. "Just kissing, huh?"

"That's my story and I'm sticking to it."

"Huh. So what happened?"

"He asked me to the Military Ball."

"Ah, a regular Cinderella story?" He took a sip of his champagne.

Sydney sighed sadly. "I thought so. Right up until I found out that he was trying to win a damn bet."

Jett lowered his glass and met her suddenly glossy glaze.

"I wasn't very sociable in school and lot of kids thought since I was so standoffish that I was a bitch. Turns out that there was pool on whether Romeo could get me to sleep with him on the night of the ball." She smiled, though it completely missed her eyes.

"And the answer is no. I didn't."

"How did you find out?"

"I overheard some girls talking in the ladies' room at the ball."

"What did you do?"

Sydney shrugged. "What any girl would do in that situation. I kicked his ass."

Chapter 16

By their main course, Sydney continued to dispense stories about her misadventures with the opposite sex, which included Bobby "Octopus Arms" Blalock at her senior ball. Quite a few of them were pretty funny—in retrospect, of course. But the one thing he was dying to know was about the first time she'd made love. *Why did men always want to know that?*

Anyway, she decided to keep that tidbit to herself. After all, it was the first date.

"So, where did you learn that move today in the simulator?" she asked, smoothly changing the subject and starting in on her third drink. "I thought you were crazy."

Jett shrugged off the compliment, but his chest puffed up a couple of inches. "I don't know. It just clicked in my head. *Go toward it.* A heat-seeking missile can speed up or slow down, but once it slows down, it can't speed up again."

"Once you head toward it, the missile slows down to wait for you."

He nodded along as she put the pieces together. "So, at the right moment you execute a perfect glide-and-roll and say '*adios.*'"

"Brilliant."

Jett stretched back in his seat. "Well, I don't want to brag."

"Of course not." She laughed at his feigned modesty and took another bite of her heavenly dish. "What about you?" she asked. "Do we even have time tonight to discuss the women in your past?"

His modest act continued as he flashed his pearly whites and averted his eyes. "There haven't been as many as you think."

"Said the spider to the fly."

He laughed. "No, no. I pretty much lived in the shadow of my older brother."

"There are two of you?" She chuckled.

"Only Xavier is a much better version, apparently."

Pain rippled across his features again and Sydney felt that instinctive pang to take him into her arms and console him.

"Anyway, my brother was the Casanova of the

family. Girls didn't notice me until after he left home for college."

Sydney's gaze sank deep into his golden eyes and a smile tugged her lips. "Bullshit."

His laugh was like a warm blanket on a chilly night and she basked in the wonderful feeling that it gave her—or was it the buzz from the wine? "You know, you can be quite charming when you want."

"Shh." He jiggled his brows. "Don't tell anyone."

"It doesn't mean that you don't have to answer the same questions."

"What questions?"

"Nice try. Who was your first love?" She took another pull from her drink and felt positively lovely.

"My first love was Halle Berry."

"C'mon," she chastised him with a pop to his hand. "You're not being serious."

"Yes, I am. Did you ever see *The Last Boy Scout?*"

Sydney folded her arms and smote him with a narrowed glare. "I told you the truth."

"All right. All right." His hands flew up in surrender. "Valerie Wexler—fourth grade. Her brothers beat me up when they found out I kissed her behind the monkey bars during PE."

"Scandalous."

"More like curiosity killed the cat." Jett's smile turned sly. "But we hooked back up in high school and were pretty serious through our junior and senior year. I thought I was going to marry her, spit out a couple of kids and drive a minivan."

Jealousy knotted Sydney's buzzing nerves as she watched how fondly he reflected on his childhood love. "What happened?"

"She went off to college, met my brother and married him."

"What?" Sydney dropped her fork and then jumped at the clatter it made. "Oh, I—I'm sorry." Was that the appropriate thing to say?

"Don't be." He shrugged and fixed a strained smile on his face. "It's all water under the bridge."

"Bullshit."

The smile turned genuine and he added a wink. "You know, I like you."

Before she had a chance to respond, their waiter placed a slice of chocolate cake before her with a lone candle.

"Joyeux anniversaire, mademoiselle," said the waiter.

Jett lifted his glass in salute. "Happy birthday, Sydney. I hope you get everything you've ever wanted."

Their eyes met and held while their glasses clinked together. How easy it would be to spend the rest of the night drowning in his eyes. Actually, there were a few things she could easily do for the rest of the night.

The renegade thought startled her and she jumped in her seat.

"What? Is something wrong?" he asked.

Her fuzzy brain couldn't process a lie so she could only manage a deer-caught-in-headlights look.

Concern etched his fine features. "Syd?"

"Huh, I was just thinking that this evening turned out pretty good. It might even be one of the best birthdays I've ever had."

"Might be?"

She hitched her shoulders. "It's in the top ten."

Jett puffed up his chest. "I think I can settle for that. Make a wish and blow out your candle."

Giddy, Sydney twitched in her seat while she thought what to wish for. The first thing to cross her mind was to finish top gun in her Special Ops training; but when she glanced across the table, another wish bubbled to the surface.

She closed her eyes and blew out the candle.

"What did you wish for?"

"If I tell you, it won't come true." She took her fork and dipped into the very rich dessert.

"Fine. Don't tell me."

Sydney smiled and tasted the cake. Instantly, she released a long moan as she closed and rolled her eyes.

Jett shifted in his seat at the erotic sound and picture she posed. Hell, for the last hour he'd done little more than imagine her draped over a massive bed of red silk, her beautiful face awash with passion. Would she submit or would she fight him for dominance? Something told him that it would be the latter.

Then again, the fight might be as hot as the sex.

Okay, now he was overreaching. There was no way this date was going to end with the two of them in bed. This was technically their first real date and Sydney Garrett was not the kind of girl to sleep with a man on the first date. Right?

Right. *God, I hope I'm wrong.*

"Here." She lifted a forkful of the cake toward him. "Have a bite."

He complied and emitted his own moan when the delicious moist dessert entered his mouth. When Sydney twitched in her chair, he was cocky enough to believe that he was having the same effect on her.

"Why don't we get out of here?"

Chapter 17

Sydney and Jett returned to Rain at the Palm.

Loose as a goose, Sydney blended seamlessly with the partying crowd. However, it wasn't until she'd downed a couple of strong margaritas that she truly let her hair down.

It turned out Jett was just as impressive on the dance floor as he was in the sky. The feel of his body bumping and rubbing against her had her worked into a fevered pitch.

She wanted him. Bad.

As Jett danced he had a hard time keeping his hands and body parts from touching and moving

across Sydney's. Her every curve called his name—
and he loved its sound.

When he'd suggested coming back to the dance
club, he'd thought it was an easy way to exorcise
his sexual frustration; unfortunately, it made it
worse. It blew his wildest dreams seeing the usually
stern and disciplined Captain Garrett so carefree, so
sexy—so damn hot.

Then, out of the blue, Sydney grabbed the front
of his shirt and jerked him forward for a mind-
blowing kiss. Once the shock subsided, Jett wrapped
his arms around her curvy figure and drew her closer.

The crowd and the music disappeared. All that
existed, all that was good and important, was locked
in his arms. Soon, her lips became an addiction he
couldn't imagine kicking.

Sydney was the first to break the kiss. When she
looked up at him, her chest heaved as though she'd
completed a marathon.

The crowd and the music returned.

"What do you say we get a room?" she asked.

He blinked, certain he'd heard her wrong. He
leaned toward her ear. "What did you say?"

She shouted back into his ear so there would be
no misunderstanding. Even then, he still couldn't
believe it.

But Sydney mistook his hesitance and began to
backpedal. "It's all right," she said, looking embarrassed. "I understand if you don't want to."

"No, no. I want to." His smile broadened. "I just want to make sure that *you* want to do this."

"Why wouldn't I want to unwrap my birthday gift?"

Jett plunked down a credit card at the reservation desk and then smiled awkwardly at the front desk clerk while Sydney giggled and nibbled on his ear. To the clerk's credit, she smiled and handed over their keys as if their behavior was normal.

"Enjoy your stay."

"Oh, we will," Sydney promised and took the keys before Jett had a chance to accept them.

It was a good thing the elevator was as quick as it was. Jett had a feeling they were just seconds away from giving the guys in surveillance quite a peep show.

They stumbled into their suite with their arms entwined and their lips locked.

Jett couldn't put into words what her body was doing to him, didn't know how it was possible to feel as if he'd found a missing part of himself. It didn't make any sense for such emotions to be elicited from a woman who challenged him as much Sydney Garrett did.

But, boy, was he loving it.

She backed into the room while he directed them toward the bed.

She dropped her purse and pulled at the buttons

of his shirt. He helped her—never once breaking their kiss. The moment her hands touched his bare chest, a growl rumbled deep within.

He slid the dress straps from her shoulders and then attacked the tiny, infuriating zipper in the back. It took some work but when he heard the small sliding sound, it was like music to his ears.

When the dress fell from her body, Jett stole a peek at what lay beneath. He was not disappointed.

Black satin hugged her curves and caused his fingers to itch. He wanted to take his time but he was impatient, as well. Decisions. Decisions.

Sydney peeled Jett's shirt from his body and felt a sharp, hungry pang at the sight of his rich caramel skin. She abandoned his lips to take a light nibble of his muscled shoulder and relished the sweet taste of him.

Finally, she bumped up against the bed and fell back onto its soft bedding. Jett smiled and then crawled on top of her. "You have no idea how long I've been wanting to do this."

"What—talk me to death?" Sydney rolled and took the top position.

He chuckled, but when she reached back and unsnapped her bra, all humor vanished. Her full, luscious breasts sat proud and high on her chest and Jett's hands reached as though he'd found the meaning of life.

They filled his hands perfectly. He squeezed and

fell in love with their softness. His mouth watered and he couldn't wait any longer to taste them.

Sydney melted when Jett's mouth settled around a hard nipple. At his gentle suckle, she thrust her head back and squirmed against his erection.

She moaned.

He groaned.

She squirmed again and dug her fingers into his strong back. Jett sucked in a startled breath and scraped his teeth across her sensitive nipple. Her eyes widened in reaction, and she thought she would come unglued from the exquisite pleasure.

"Oh, I see how you like it." Jett chuckled and then raked his teeth again across her soft flesh. "You like things a little rough."

A wicked laugh tumbled from Sydney's lips. "I don't like anything 'little.'"

Their eyes locked and the temperature in the room climbed another ten degrees. In one smooth movement, Jett swung Sydney back onto the bed and pinned her wrists above her head with one hand.

"Challenge accepted," he growled and then branded her with his hot mouth. He loved the way she whimpered and writhed beneath him as his free hand returned to her breast. This time he was rough, rolling and pinching at her nipple. She bucked against him.

"You like that, baby?"

"More," she rasped.

Lust surged through his body as he thrust his tongue deep into her waiting mouth. His hand abandoned her breast to rake off her panties.

Sydney freed one hand from his grip and raged a semiwar to relieve him of his pants. It was awkward work, just using his one hand and her one hand, but they managed to get the job done.

She shifted her weight and tried to roll him over, but he would have none of that and the two wrestled for control.

Jett won by standing up from the bed, pulling her legs up with him and slinging them over opposite shoulders.

Sydney thrust her hands over her head and gripped the bed's sheets. She blinked when she realized she was upside down. However, her amazement gave way to mind-bending pleasure when the heat of his mouth warmed her other set of lips.

She twisted and quivered; his mouth was too intense and his tongue unrelenting. Moaning and whimpering, she tried to crawl away, but she was lost in a sensual abyss. She cried out and then had trouble sustaining air in her lungs.

Jett released her legs and helped her do a back flip onto the bed. If she thought about a temporary reprieve, she was sadly mistaken. She pulled herself up on all fours, but he reappeared and pinned her back down to the bed.

She fought him, wanting desperately to do something for or to him, but there was no escaping his grip this time. She bucked at his rough handling, her rump wiggling against his iron-hard erection.

She loved every moment of the struggle for dominance, even though she was on the losing end—or was she?

"I know what I need to do with you," Jett rasped. He had to release her in order to reach for the pillows. When he did, Sydney wasted no time scrambling around so she could finally see her "birthday gift."

And what a *big* gift it was.

"Oh, my." Her eyes widened as she greedily reached for him. She slid her hands down the hard yet silky shaft and cooed in wonderment.

He sucked in a sharp breath and placed his hand on her shoulder to pull her back. However, this time, Sydney got the upper hand when she gave him a deep, intimate kiss.

Jett dropped the pillow and reared his head back. It wouldn't hurt to give up some control, he reasoned. Shortly after, he was unable to think at all. He could only feel…and what he felt was too wonderful for words or to be believed.

A test of stamina ensued and, after a long while, Jett had a sinking suspicion he was just on the verge of losing. So he did what any other man would do: he cheated. In one big burst of strength, he extracted Sydney from her loving worship, plopped her back over onto her stomach and snatched the pillowcases off the pillow.

Faster than the average cowboy could hogtie a calf, Jett strapped Sydney's arms to the bedpost. When he was done, he sat and watched her lovely rear wiggle and jiggle as she struggled to break free.

"I wasn't finished," she whined, already beginning to settle down.

"Neither am I," he promised and then stood from the bed.

"Wait. Where are you going?"

The room filled with his rich laughter. "Don't worry. I'm not leaving you."

She listened as his feet padded away and hoped he was a man of his word. Not because she didn't want the cleaning staff to find her in this position, but because she needed satisfaction to the erotic ache of his making.

At his return, a wicked smile curved his lips.

"Did you miss me?" he asked, climbing back onto the bed.

She wiggled again. "What do you think?"

She sighed and purred at the feel of Jett's large hands roaming and caressing her upturned tush, her inner thigh, and then finally grazing the V of curls between her legs.

Sydney spread her legs wide, hoping to give him better access to her pulsing bud.

"That's right. Open up, baby." He bent forward

and kissed the curve of her back. His hand teased her three sensitive spots while her legs slid wider.

"Please," she begged when she could no longer stand the torture.

"Please what, baby?" He kissed her back again.

"Please, I need you," she panted.

"You do?" He slid a finger deep into her warm, damp heat.

Sydney's head lifted off the bed as she emitted a long sigh. When Jett's hand remained still a wild anxiousness took hold of her and she shifted her weight so she could rock her body against his hand.

"That's right, baby. Show me what you can do."

That was all the encouragement she needed to find her own frenzied rhythm. As a reward, he slipped in another finger. While his light kisses turned into small bites, Sydney could feel and hear how wet she was and the small kisses he rained across her back had her mind soaring through the clouds.

Her orgasm shook her body like an earthquake and her legs trembled with aftershocks.

"No rest for the weary, my love." He positioned himself behind her and ripped open the condom packet he'd retrieved from his pants pocket. Quickly, he slid on the latex and clamped his hands around her waist for support as he entered her with one deep thrust.

Sydney gasped and pulled on her restraints.

However, whenever she moved her tight body, Jett's grip tightened and his toes curled.

This was what he'd dreamed of since the first day he'd met her. Now that their bodies were joined together, he became an animal. Desperate and hungry.

"Oh, yes," she croaked, thrusting back in the same frantic pace he'd set. "Don't stop. Don't you dare stop."

A light sheen of sweat covered their bodies and caused the already slick silk sheets to stick.

"Are you coming, baby?"

Was she ever! She'd never had sex like this in her life. She'd only dreamed of it and couldn't believe that it was actually happening.

Sydney's sharp, soft sighs quickened. Her next orgasm unfurled and slammed into her soul while tears of joy rolled down her eyes.

Teeth clenched, Jett was mindless to all but their thunderous rhythm and sparks of fireworks. With one final thrust, lightning flashed behind his eyes and his body exploded like a thunderclap.

Panting, he unwound the pillowcases from the bedpost and then collapsed down beside her. "That was—"

"Incredible." Sydney slithered close and then curled up beside him.

Jett turned onto his side so he could meet her gaze. "*You* are incredible."

She smiled. "You're not so bad yourself."

"One does what one can."

They laughed, and another round of lovemaking ensued where they tried to take things slowly. But it didn't work out. This time, Jett found himself submissive beneath her.

When Sydney was done, the new lovers snuggled together and sprinkled kisses over one another. In between, they talked about their pasts, their losses and even shared some hopes and dreams for the future.

Jett held her while he whispered sweet nothings. He couldn't believe the jewel he'd unearthed. Somehow, some way, this woman had touched a part of him he'd never known existed. Now that he'd found her, he was going to hold on to her at all cost.

At long last, Sydney's eyes grew heavy with sleep just as sunlight streamed into the room. Jett Colton was the best birthday gift she could have hoped for and one that she had no intention of ever returning.

Chapter 18

Sydney's birthday date turned into a birthday weekend extravaganza where the two new lovers rarely ventured outside their hotel suite at the Palms. The bed, the Jacuzzi, the shower—Jett and Sydney made love everywhere and still couldn't get enough.

When they returned to Nellis Air Base late Sunday night, Weasel caught sight of them sneaking in together and noted that Sydney wore the same dress she'd left in on Friday night. That was all it took to set tongues wagging.

For the first time in her life, Sydney had acted without thinking of the consequences. At every turn, some jerk had a snide remark about her and Jett. She and Jett agreed to deny the charges and claim only to be friends, but no one bought their story. The teasing and snickering grew so bad Sydney feared that even Major Maxwell would have to address the issue.

After three weeks had passed, however, she finally allowed herself to breathe a sigh of relief.

Niecy remained silent, though her expression seemed permanently pinched with disappointment.

"I want to see you tonight," Jett whispered behind her as they marched in the back of the line toward their hangar for today's flight test.

Sydney glanced around in fear that one of their colleagues had overheard him. When it looked as if they were in the clear, she hissed back, "I don't think that's such a good idea."

"Let me rephrase that. I *need* you tonight."

Sydney fought the smile tugging at her lips. "The answer is still no."

"C'mon. I want to try that thing you did with the—"

"Jett!" She stopped and swiveled around to pierce him with a daring glare. Judging by the smile on his face, he mistook her darkening face as embarrassment instead of anger.

"Captain Garrett and Lieutenant Colton," Major Maxwell barked. "Do we have a problem?"

Now Sydney's face colored with embarrassment. She turned around and faced her squadron only to discover them in line formation before the hangar, their eyes glued to her and Jett. "Uh, no, sir." She saluted. "There is no problem, sir."

"Good." Maxwell folded his arms. "Then maybe you two *lovebirds* would like to join the rest of the class?"

Completely humiliated, Sydney saluted again.

"Yes, sir," she and Jett boomed in unison and raced to fall in line.

Maxwell paced before the small group with his irritation still etched on his face. "Today, class, we're going to begin training in the B-2 Spirit Stealth Bomber. The B-2 is a low-observable, strategic, long-range, heavy bomber capable of penetrating sophisticated and dense air-defense shields. It is capable of all-altitude attack missions up to fifty thousand feet, and has the ability to fly to any point in the world within hours."

Sydney's eyes roamed over the sleek black plane, and she could feel the familiar nervous anxiety race through her veins.

"The cockpit accommodates a two-man crew. It is equipped with an electronic flight instrumentation system, which displays flight, engine and sensor data and avionics systems and weapons status. The pilot can choose to activate the appropriate selection of flight and mission equipment for takeoff mode, go-to-war mode and landing mode by using a simple three-way switch."

The entire squadron absorbed every word Major

Maxwell said about the B-2 stealth plane. The plane's most impressive capability, though it had many, was its ability to avoid radar detection. Sydney couldn't wait to get behind the controls of the high supersonic aircraft.

"Okay," Major Maxwell said, ending his speech. "I need everyone to team up. "Captain Garrett?"

Sydney snapped to a salute. "Yes, sir."

"Pick someone other than your boyfriend."

She blinked and worked her jaw, but actual words eluded her.

"Is that a problem, Captain Garrett?"

"Sir, no, sir."

"Good. Everyone strap up."

There was an unmistakable titter of laughter within the ranks while everyone selected their partner. Sydney somehow found the strength to keep her head held high as she stepped out of formation. She didn't dare glance in Jett's direction, even though she could feel his heavy gaze on her.

She ended up teaming with Lieutenant Johnson while Jett looked disgruntled to partner with Captain Post. Strange, but Sydney noticed Johnson seemed distant—aloof even. Whenever he spotted her with Jett, she was sure she read disappointment in his features. Had Niecy been right about him? Had he been interested in her?

The day's mission was just to log time in the B-2 Spirit, but that didn't mean the pilots didn't get their chance to test what a forty-five-million-dollar plane could do.

As much as Sydney loved the F-16, it took her less than two seconds to find a tender spot for the B-2. The moment she was strapped in, she felt as if she'd been cast in a science fiction movie. The huge, intimidating plane was not made of metal but of a composite material that reduced the overall weight of the aircraft.

At liftoff, Sydney couldn't believe the speed and the power the plane exuded. Rocketing at supersonic speed and maneuvering this way and that felt more like an aphrodisiac than a training mission.

Everyone felt it.

The men were juiced with extra testosterone and Sydney's legs quivered as badly as they had when she'd lain writhing beneath Jett in their silk-sheet haven at the Palms.

Now she needed him.

When she was stripping out of her G-suit in the locker room, she quickly jotted a note. However, she chose the wrong time to pass it to him when they returned to the classroom.

"Thank you, Captain Garrett." Major Maxwell plucked the folded paper from her hands. "I'm sure this is an interesting bit of literature that the rest of the class would enjoy."

Sydney groaned and shrank into her chair as another titter of laughter encircled her. To her great relief, Major Maxwell didn't open the letter and read it aloud as he'd threatened. Instead, he continued his lecture on the B-2 Spirit for another hour.

When class finally ended, Maxwell instructed her and Jett to stay seated.

Once the room had cleared, Major Maxwell pulled up a seat. "Does this place look like a high school to you?"

"No, sir," Sydney and Jett barked back.

"I think it does." He pulled Sydney's letter from his pants pocket and carefully unfolded it.

Sydney fought the urge to dive across her desk and snatch the paper from his hands. Instead, she sat there and watched him as he read all the things Sydney wanted to do to Jett when she next got him alone.

As long as it took, Sydney was certain he'd read her fantasy a few times. When he was done, he handed the letter over to Lieutenant Colton.

"You sound very talented, Captain Garrett."

"Yes, sir," she responded automatically, but when Major Maxwell's bushy eyebrows lifted with blatant humor, she realized what she'd said. "Uh, I mean— no, sir." That wasn't right either, was it?

Major Maxwell lifted a silencing hand to let her off the hook. "I'm old school," he admitted. "If you ask me, integrating the sexes in the forces has turned out to be one big headache. I recognize that you two are consenting adults and you are free to do whatever it is you do behind closed doors, but when you're on my time, I expect your best in the sky as well as the classroom. Do I make myself clear?"

"Yes, sir," Sydney and Jett chorused.

"Very well." Major Maxwell stood. "Dismissed."

"We have to cool it," Sydney declared, marching toward the housing. Tears of humiliation burned the backs of her eyes.

"C'mon. It's not that serious." Jett chuckled behind her. "We just have to play things a little closer to the vest. That's all." He snuck a quick pinch of her butt.

Sydney nearly jumped out of her skin. "What the hell is the matter with you?" She whipped her head around to see who was watching. "Don't touch me," she muttered, and then quickened her pace toward her destination.

"Aw. Loosen up. Class is over."

Sydney shook her head. How could she have forgotten how different they were? Jett was a great pilot, but his devil-may-care attitude would likely limit his advancement more than anything. She didn't just want to be a fighter pilot; she wanted to be *the best*. That's all she'd ever wanted.

"Syd?"

She stopped and turned to look at him, fully intending to break it off, but the moment she met his beautiful golden gaze, she realized she'd rather rip out her own tongue than to break things off.

Jett seemed to know his power over her and slid

on his goofiest smile. "I promise from now on to be on my best behavior."

The war between her head and her heart raged. For the first time ever, logic lost the war. "No more sexual advances in class."

"I promise." He stepped forward as if he was about to embrace her.

"And no more improper touching in public."

Jett frowned. "In public—ever?"

Okay, she didn't like that one, either. "Not on the base."

He thought it over. "Agreed. As long as you don't pass any more sexually explicit notes in class."

An image of Major Maxwell's lobster-red face as he read her letter flashed before her eyes. "That is definitely a deal."

"Good. It's Friday night. How about I meet you at Studio 54 about midnight?"

"I don't know." She groaned, desperately wanting to say no, but dying to say yes. "What if we're seen?"

"So? After today the whole squad definitely knows we're seeing each other. We just agreed to be professional *on base*. Now, what happens in Vegas—"

"I know. I know."

"So, what do you say?"

She hesitated. There was one week left of training and there was no way she could resist him that long.

"Who knows," Jett said in low whisper. "I might even let you see me naked."

"Hey," she reprimanded with a wave of her finger. "You promised."

"Midnight?"

She drew a deep breath and finally gave in. "Midnight."

Studio 54, located at the spectacular MGM Grand, proved to be just as breathtaking as Rain. The moment Sydney entered the building it was as if she'd been transported back in time to the infamous nightclub of the seventies.

"Care to dance?" a male voice inquired from behind her.

She turned around to refuse the offer but stopped in her tracks when she realized it was Lieutenant Johnson.

"Oh, are you talking to me again?"

He shrugged casually. "Sorry about that, but I guess my jealousy got the best of me."

Stunned, she blinked up at him.

"But if you ever change your mind about Colton, I hope you look me up."

"I thought you were *my* date this evening?" Jett asked, brushing his body against hers.

Sydney jumped and then turned toward him. "Uh, Lieutenant Johnson just asked me—"

"It's all right," Johnson interrupted. "Maybe another time." He winked and then disappeared into the crowd.

"I don't like that guy," Jett said.

Sydney said nothing. She was too stunned. Instead, she looped her arms around Jett's neck and tuned out the upbeat dance track booming from the DJ box; instead she and Jett moved as though grooving to a slow jam.

"You're all mine," Jett whispered. The moment he'd said the words he realized he meant them. So rarely had life given him something to hold on to, and now that he held this gem he had no desire to ever let her go.

Something about the way Jett looked at Sydney had her reevaluating her life plan. Whenever she was in his arms, she envisioned the white picket fence and two and a half children. Such things were alien to her. There was something magical about the night as they stood in the center of the floor with smoke billowing around.

They danced for hours and then at the bar, Jett talked her into trying her first ever Hurricane.

"Trust me. You're going to love it," he promised.

And she did—at least the first one. On the second drink, her whole world turned blurry. There was more dancing, more laughing. Vaguely, she remembered them moving to the casino floor where there was quite a bit of questionable betting going on. But none of that explained how she woke up Saturday morning in an MGM suite naked…except for the silver band on her left hand.

Survival, Evasion and Resistance

Chapter 19

Tuesday, July 4, 2006: 1900 hours. Somewhere in North Korea

Sydney grew concerned about infection in her left leg as she prepared for her first night in the strange territory. Having not received so much as static on her radio, she was finding it hard to remain hopeful about a search-and-rescue team.

As dire as her situation was, there was nothing for her to do but to sit and wait—and think. But thinking led to remembering and she didn't want to continue wallowing in the past. What purpose did it serve other than to depress her?

She'd loved. She'd lost. She needed to get over it. Of course that was how Sydney felt now. In ten minutes that declaration was subject to change. In a place where the minutes crawled like hours it was hard not to think about the what-ifs.

Now that night had descended, she had to get moving. Nighttime was the best time to travel and she needed to get to a place where she could get better reception on her radio. But when she tried to stand, the pain in her leg returned tenfold and it took everything she had not to cry out.

Slumping back down to the cold earth, Sydney tried to catch her breath. After a long while, when the pain had finally dulled a bit, she took another look at her red, black and blue injury. She winced and sucked in a deep breath as she pulled pieces of what looked like scrap metal from her leg.

When she was through, she was light-headed and the flow of blood coursing down her leg increased. From her survival vest, she withdrew a small medical kit and a tourniquet to help stop the flow of blood. After doctoring her leg, a part of her argued that she shouldn't try walking again, but another part, a strong part, argued that she couldn't stay put.

After several more tries, Sydney collapsed back to the ground, tired and sweaty. Before she could give in to self-pity, a sound caught her ear.

Don't move.

Her breath wedged in her throat and her heart

pounded so fast she feared that any moment it would explode out of her chest. She heard the unmistakable sounds of heavy footfalls racing in her direction, and she hunkered down and retrieved her Beretta.

Is this it? Is this how it's all going to end?

A somber image of her mother answering the door to a U.S. Air Force officer and chaplain surfaced in her mind. Would she handle this news with the same quiet decorum as she had when her husband was killed—or would she break down at the loss of her only daughter?

The spouses and parents of military personnel are more than aware of the dangers of military life, but no one is ever really prepared.

Leaves crunched and branches snapped beneath the runners' feet.

They're getting close.

If it were soldiers, she had no choice but to believe they would be hostile as well as unpredictable. The night grew darker and she had to strain to make anything out, but then at last, a short figure burst into view.

Sydney's heart stopped at the sight of a Korean soldier bearing down on her hiding spot with his weapon drawn.

The North American Aerospace Defense Command, which monitors the skies for threats to national security, remained on heightened alert while everyone from the president of the United States to the U.N. Security Council tried to guess whether the international community was on the brink of a world war.

A North Korean foreign ministry official had confirmed the test firing of one long-range missile and five short-range rockets. All six had failed. There were no reports about the surface-to-air missiles launched at two American F-16s. That tidbit was suspiciously absent from their reports.

Jett, along with the rest of the Rescue Combat Air Patrol, returned to base after hours of patrolling the DMZ. Despite the seriousness of North Korea's provocation, the U.N. Security Council emergency session urged more dialogue with the country instead of military action. In short, permission to cross the DMZ was denied—especially without a signal from the missing pilot.

Jett knew the five steps in the recovery system: report, locate, support, recover and return. The military couldn't rescue someone without knowing the individual's *exact* location.

What if she's dead?

The question stabbed his heart, and he fought like hell to keep the tears from burning his eyes. Life kept handing him one bad deal after another. He should have stopped her from walking out of his life. After a lifetime of begging his father to love him, he couldn't bring himself to do it all again with Sydney.

He expected her to know him—to know his heart. The fact she believed that he would purposely hurt her still tore at him.

"I heard you were being deployed here."

Jett swiveled around before entering the locker room. "Major Johnson." He straightened his shoulders. "Long time no see. I'm glad you survived your close call this morning."

Johnson dropped his gaze. "I wish I wasn't the only one."

"She's not dead," Jett snapped angrily. Truthfully, he didn't know who he was trying to convince, Johnson or himself.

A sad smile ghosted around Johnson's lips. "I pray you're right. She a great asset to the 51st. She's also one hell of a woman. Of course, I'm sure that you don't know much about that."

Jett stepped forward, ready to pound the guy's mouth in, but Johnson simply held his hands up in surrender. "I'm not going to fight you. You're not worth it."

The words, so similar to what his father used to say, cut Jett to the quick.

"She loves you, you know," Johnson added. "Even after all this time, she still loves you. Go figure." Shaking his head, he turned and walked away.

Jett watched him leave, wishing that the man had fought him instead of causing more injury to his already battered heart.

In the locker room, Jett released his tears while standing beneath the shower's pulsing flow. The memories were no longer bittersweet; they were just painful.

He shut off the water and dressed without having any memory of doing so. But when he stepped out of his squadron and into the muggy night, his gaze flew to the full moon hanging above his head.

Was it too much to hope that Sydney's gaze was upon the same moon? His lips quirked at his use of the word *hope*. Apparently, he wasn't ready to give up on the elusive emotion.

"Sydney, if you're out there, just hold on, baby. I'm going to find you." He wanted to say more but his raw emotion lodged in his throat. He wanted to pray but feared he'd forgotten how. Maybe he could bargain with God, promise to be a better man—do away with his pride.

In the end, he didn't know what to do.

Jett closed his eyes, and, for the briefest of moments, the night's slight wind felt more like a woman's caress. Concentrating, he focused on the memory of waking up next to Mrs. James Colton. It was the happiest day of his life.

Chapter 20

Jett moaned in his sleep and pulled the pliant, soft body next to him closer. He could definitely get used to waking up this way every morning for the rest of his life—just as he could get used to Sydney's smile and laughter. Captain Garrett challenged his mind, but Hurricane Sydney did things to his body and soul that he dared not name.

She stirred in his arms and Jett nuzzled her neck. "Good morning, sunshine," he whispered.

Her lyrical laugh danced around his foggy head and he slid on a sly smile.

"Is that a gun in your pocket or are you just happy to see me?" She laughed.

"Uh, I'm not wearing any pants so what do you think?" He rubbed his morning hard-on against her adorable backside and roamed a hand over the cliffs of her breasts, down the flat plane of her belly and then glided it into the soft down between her legs.

Sydney sighed and opened her legs wider to give him better access. "Is this what you're looking for?"

"Oh, yes." Jett slipped his fingers into her slick passage and caressed the pink bud with slow, tender strokes. "I want all of it."

"Come and get it, Soldier," she half dared and half teased him.

"Yes, sir, Captain." He entered her from behind and had trouble trying to keep his eyes from rolling to the back of his head. This is what it meant to find the missing half of oneself. It had to be. Sydney's tight body sheathed him perfectly.

"Oh, you feel so good." She tightened her vaginal muscles and rocked back against him.

Jett deepened his thrust and couldn't comprehend how each time he entered her was better than the last. The thought didn't make sense, since each thrust was as close to heaven as he would ever get.

Wanting a better view of her beautiful face, Jett abandoned the spoon position to roll her onto her back and jack her legs high over his shoulders where his thrust quickly morphed into a fierce pounding. He wanted—no, needed—to get as deep as he could, to touch her soul as much as she touched his.

"Yes…oh, yes…" Sydney panted, urging him on.

His body devoured hers. His mind transported him to another place that could only be described as spiritual.

Sydney released a long, throaty cry as her body quivered deliciously and Jett could no longer maintain his control.

"Oh, Syd, I love you," he chanted as he erupted violently inside her. "I love you, I love you."

Sydney clung to his broad back as he collapsed against her. As a reward, she peppered sweet kisses along his sweaty brow.

However, Jett's brain kicked into instant replay. He realized what he'd said during his climax and he registered that Sydney had not repeated the words to him.

"That was a wonderful remedy for a hangover," she whispered lightly, caressing his back and muscled butt cheeks. "I had this wild dream last night." She chuckled under her breath.

"If it was a nasty dream, I want details." He joined in her laughter and hoped he was successful in masking his hurt.

"No, it was just crazy, yet at the same time it seemed so real."

Jett rolled over onto his side and gathered her close. She might not share his feelings now, but in time, she would. "You have me curious now. What was it about?"

Sydney shook her head and snuggled closer. "No. You'll just laugh."

"I won't laugh."

Again, she shook her head but then climbed up from her comfortable nook to straddle him.

"Ooh." Jett felt himself grow hard again. "Was this a part of the dream?"

"No, silly." She splayed her hands flat across his chest and froze.

Jett tensed at her stricken expression and sat up. "What is it, baby? What's wrong?"

"Oh, my God." She tried to scramble off his lap, but Jett locked an arm around her waist to hold her in place. "Oh, my God."

"What? What?"

Sydney lifted her left hand as her features distorted into shock. "It wasn't a dream."

Jett's gaze slowly followed to her hand and the simple silver band that he'd purchased from an Elvis Presley impersonator.

"We're…we're…"

"Married," he finished for her. Did she truly believe it had been a dream?

She blinked as if seized by a sudden case of epilepsy and her voice rose to newly discovered notes. "We—we can't be married." She successfully won her freedom and leaped to her feet, but wobbled for balance. "What the hell were we thinking?"

He hesitated as he recalled the events of the previous night. Admittedly there were a few holes in his memory, but he certainly remembered Sydney asking *him* to marry her.

Sydney raced from the bed and began picking up her clothes that were scattered across the room.

"What are you doing?" he asked.

"What does it look like?" She snatched one of her shoes off the top of the television set. "Married? Me? Us?"

Jett winced but tried not to read too much into her statement.

"I mean, we hardly know each other," she ranted. "You know what I mean?" Her large, inquiring eyes sought his and then waited for affirmation.

He was able to give it and he was at a loss on what to do.

Sydney stopped darting about the room and eyed him suspiciously. "Why are you so quiet?"

Jett shrugged and casually leaned back against the pillows. "I just fail to see what the problem is. You asked me to marry you. I said yes and we raced out and got married." He slid on a smile. "If my memory serves me correctly, we even consummated the marriage quite a few times, too."

"*I* asked you?"

"You were adorable, too." He winked.

She stared at him as if he'd lost his mind.

"C'mon." He shrugged again and climbed out of bed. "Being married to me isn't the worst thing in the world."

"How could we get married without a license?" she asked, ignoring his last statement.

"You made sure we got one of those, too."

She looked faint. "I need to sit down."

Jett took the fact that she hadn't succeeded in fleeing the suite as a good sign. "Frankly, I think we should upgrade to the honeymoon suite," he joked.

"This isn't funny," she mumbled and hid her face behind her hands. "We have to find a judge or something."

Her words were like a punch in the gut. "If that's what you want to do…"

Sydney jerked her head up and glanced over at him. "What I *want* to do? That's the only thing *to* do, isn't it?"

"Yeah, sure. Of course." This time, he glanced around and began gathering his stuff.

She watched him. "Are you upset?"

"No," he barked a little too loudly. "I'm going to jump in the shower." Without another word, he walked into the bathroom and slammed the door.

Sydney jumped and stared at the door. She listened as the water came on in the shower. The need to go to him was nearly overpowering, but the truth of the matter was she was scared.

She had never been in a serious relationship in her life. Her career had been all she lived and breathed for. Now, she was with a man who obviously affected her thinking.

I proposed to him?

Maybe she did remember something like that. She was on a roll at the craps table and—she shook her head. *What the hell was I doing playing craps?*

She glanced down at her hand and stared at the simple silver band. "Love me tender, love me sweet, never let me go," she sang softly and then realized what she was doing.

Married?

A smile fluttered across her lips. As she allowed the reality to settle in, it didn't seem so outrageous as it had ten minutes ago. The idea of Jett belonging to her or her belonging to him sent a nice little thrill through her.

She remained on the bed while her thoughts chased each other in circles in her head. Next, she analyzed her emotions, but there were too many. Jett challenged her, annoyed her and even angered her. Yet at the same time, he was funny, cheesy, intelligent, sexy, sensitive, a great kisser—and damn good in bed.

She cared for him.

She liked him—no, that wasn't right. What she felt was much deeper than that. Sydney glanced up at the door and finally stood from the bed. Entering the bathroom, her gaze cut toward Jett's fuzzy figure behind the shower's glass door.

Jett kept his head low beneath the showerhead and didn't seem to notice her entry.

My husband.

Her body tingled as she moved toward him and then opened the door. His beautiful eyes that she'd come to love smiled back at her.

"It's about time you showed up."

Chapter 21

"You're what?" Steven blasted into the phone. "When...? Who...? What in the hell were you thinking?"

Sydney held the receiver away from her ear but had no trouble hearing her brother rant and rave. "Look, I know you're upset—"

"Me? What do you think this is going to do to Mom?"

She didn't have to think too hard for that answer; her impromptu marriage would devastate her mother.

"You're her only daughter," Steven reminded her—as though she'd forgotten. "She's been planning your marriage since you were in diapers."

"I know. I know." She glanced around the empty hotel suite. Jett had volunteered to retrieve the overnight bag from her car. He'd only been gone for a few minutes and already she missed him.

"Who in the hell did you marry? Please say not some bum you found on the street."

"That's not funny."

"Good. I wasn't trying to be."

A long pause hung in the air and Sydney figured it was safe to place the phone back against her ear.

"Well?" her brother asked. "Who is he?"

"His name is James Colton."

"Colton. Colton. Why does that name sound familiar?"

Sydney cleared her throat. "Lieutenant Jett Colton."

"The *asshole* that kissed you a couple of months ago in class?"

She shrugged and fidgeted with the phone cord. "He's not an asshole." The last thing Sydney expected was the sudden roar of laughter. "Stop. It's not funny."

"Oh, yes, it is," Steven argued through his mirth. "I don't know this guy, but I have to respect his game."

"You're doing your male bonding thing a little early, aren't you?"

"Seems to me I'm late."

"Fine. Fine." She rolled her eyes in annoyance. "Chuckle it up. You're probably just upset that I beat you to the altar. Speaking of which, when is the big day?"

At last, Steven's laughter faded to a light titter, and then collapsed into silence.

Sydney sucked in a gasp with the realization that she had wandered into a conversational land mine. "Oh, Steven, I'm so sorry."

"There's nothing to be sorry about. I haven't asked her."

"What?"

"I chickened out," he confessed, each word heavier than the last. "I'm still walking around with the damn ring in my pocket." He tried to laugh again but failed miserably.

Sydney opened her mouth and then closed it.

"Everything was perfect—dinner, music, romantic candlelight—and I froze." He paused. "Suddenly I was seized with all these what-ifs. You know what I mean?"

She did but she remained silent.

"What if Corrine isn't the one? What if there's something better out there? What if I'm not as good a husband and father as Dad was? Sometimes I wish I was more like you," he said. "Maybe you should've been the oldest."

"Me? Why?"

That awkward laughter returned. "Because you're always so damn sure of yourself."

She blinked, too stunned to speak.

"You and Dad—analytical and brave to a fault," he said. "You've always known what you wanted and how to go about achieving it."

Is that truly how he sees me?

"Me?" he continued. "I roam from place to place, trying to *find* myself. You've known who you were all along."

"Steven—"

"Take this marriage thing."

"Which wasn't planned," she reminded him.

"But you did it. You saw something you wanted and you went after it."

He lost her on that. "I was drunk out of my mind."

"Were you…? Or are you just using that as an excuse? You were attracted to that Colton guy back in July. Then fate tossed you together again at Nellis…and you set a plan in motion."

Sydney's grip tightened on the phone.

"Syd, I know you. I know no man can kiss you unless *you* want to be kissed—take 'Octopus Arms' Blalock, for example. You wouldn't have accepted a dinner date with Colton on or off your birthday if you didn't want to be with him. And you certainly wouldn't have married him—drunk or sober— without *wanting* to marry him. Am I right?"

Her denial crested her tongue but wouldn't fall.

"The funny thing is, I bet he has no clue that you were the hunter in all of this."

There were disadvantages in having someone know you too well, Sydney realized.

"You love him, don't you?"

Since the first time I saw him.

"It's okay. You don't have to answer that," Steven said quietly. "Like I said—I know you."

The suite's door opened and Jett breezed inside holding up her bag. "I hate to say it, but you can get dressed now," he joked.

Sydney stood up. "Steven, I have to go."

This time her brother fell silent.

Sydney turned her back toward Jett and whispered into the phone. "Don't tell Mom. Let me do it."

"As you should. I'll see you at the graduation ceremony."

She nodded against the phone as she turned back to face Jett and realized that there was one more thing that she needed to say to her brother before she hung up. "Steven?"

"Yes?"

"About that thing you asked a moment ago."

"About whether you love this Colton guy?"

"Yeah, that."

"What about it?"

She turned away again and lowered her voice. "The answer is—with all my heart."

"Hey, Marcus!" Weasel shouted across the Touch & Go flight kitchen. "You have a marker to settle, man." He strolled across the food service dining area with a large grin plastered across his face. "Time to pay up, man."

Niecy pulled her attention away from Lieutenant Vaughn's flirting to see what Weasel was shouting about. She watched as Captain Marcus Blocker sighed and rolled his eyes and then reached into his pocket.

"That damn Weasel made a killing off that pool," Lieutenant Vaughn grumbled into his iced tea.

"What pool?" she asked.

Blocker placed a wad of cash into Weasel's hand and then watched the man dramatically lick his fingers and count the dough.

"Uh, nothing," Vaughn backtracked. "It was nothing."

Niecy's head whipped around, and she could tell by the way Vaughn's normally café-au-lait complexion darkened that it was definitely *something*. "You have a secret," she accused, inching closer and staring into his eyes. "You can tell me. I can keep a secret."

Starved, Jett and Sydney realized that they couldn't live off sex alone. After another shower, the new husband and wife went in search of nourishment just in time for dinner.

The silver bands adorning their fingers had become the elephants in the room. There was no more talk about annulments or divorce, but neither had they sat down to discuss what exactly they were going to do.

However, it was clear they *wanted* to talk about it—but where to begin? As time ticked on and the compliments on each other's sexual prowess waned, Sydney took the elephant by the trunk.

"What's your favorite color?" Sydney blurted out and then took a bite of her steak.

"Excuse me?"

She shrugged while she mentally agreed that it was an odd question. "I figured if I'm going to be married to someone, I should at least know what his favorite color is."

Jett actually looked embarrassed before he nodded. "Very well." He dabbed his mouth with his napkin and leaned back in his seat. "Coral."

She blinked. "Come again? Coral?"

He nodded. "It's a nice warm color. It makes me feel happy whenever I see it."

She blinked again.

"You asked."

"I guess that's what I get." She shook her head and returned her attention to her meal.

"What about you? What's your favorite color?"

"Blue."

He looked unimpressed. "Oh."

Sydney frowned. "What?"

"Oh, nothing. Nothing."

After studying him a moment, she decided to let it go.

"It's just that there are all sorts of shades of blue," he lamented. "Blue doesn't tell me anything."

"What are you—a closet decorator?"

"Very funny. What shade?"

"I figured that would be obvious—sky-blue."

"Good point." He laughed and reached across the table for her hand.

"What am I going to do with you?" she asked suddenly. What would she do with a husband?

"Hopefully a lot more of what you've been doing to me." He winked. "I sort of like it…a lot."

A waiter walked by their table and Sydney blushed, afraid that Jett's words had been overheard.

"Favorite sport?" he asked.

"Football."

Right answer. "Team?"

"I'm a Georgia peach. Atlanta Falcons all the way."

Now he had no doubts. He was in love. "Sydney Garrett—"

"Garrett-Colton," she corrected.

"Hyphenated?"

Her eyes lowered to their joined hands. "I don't want to lose my father's name."

"Fair enough." He nodded and then slid the silver ring from her finger.

Her gaze shot back up to his. What was he doing? What did this mean?

Calmly, quietly, Jett eased out of his chair and then lowered onto one knee beside her. A buzz of whispers surrounded them while a delightful warmth spread through every inch of her body.

"Sydney Garrett-Colton, will you stay married to me?"

Her breath caught in her chest while her vision blurred. "Yes," she answered in a rush. "I would love to stay married to you."

Jett's hands trembled as he slid the ring back onto her finger. When he did so, he was certain his heart exploded with more love than he thought possible.

Applause filled the restaurant when Sydney wrapped her arms around him and kissed him soundly on the lips. They were doing things backward, he knew, but that was all right with him. They had the rest of their lives to get know each other.

Chapter 22

At midnight, Sydney followed Jett's car back to Nellis Air Base feeling as light as a cloud. Her smile grew wider whenever her gaze bounced from the road to the beautiful silver band around her finger.

The funny thing is, I bet he has no clue that you were the hunter in all of this.

Sydney nibbled on her lower lip. It was okay for a woman to be the hunter every once in a while, she reasoned. The important thing was she had married the man she wanted.

Entering the last week of their training, she and Jett had agreed to keep their marriage a secret from the squadron but would tell the appropriate parties of the marriage shortly after graduation. It would take a little time, but then surely the powers that be would deploy them to the same air base.

After training, Sydney's next deployment was Osan Air Base in South Korea. In truth, she was hoping to remain stateside a little longer, especially now that she and Jett needed to lay a stronger foundation for a real marriage.

"I wish that you would at least let me walk you to your door," Jett complained when they climbed out of their separate vehicles.

The base was quiet as a tomb but that didn't mean they were safe from prying eyes.

Sydney smiled as she retrieved her travel bag from the trunk. "I *want* you walk me to my door."

"You do?" He reached for her bag, but she pulled it away from his grasp.

"Yes. But we made a deal, remember?"

Jett's handsome features morphed into an adorable lost-puppy-dog look. She resisted all of thirty seconds before she approached and leaned up on her toes and kissed him.

"Kissing wasn't a part of the deal." He glided his arm around her small waist.

"I guess I slipped up. Sue me," she whispered and then kissed him again. This time it was a long, soulful kiss that sent heat clear down to her toes. When the kiss ended, she sighed and laid her head against his chest. "Are we crazy? Can this really work?"

"I sure hope so." Jett stepped back and tilted up her chin. For a long moment, he gazed in her eyes. "We haven't known each other long and I can't explain how or when it happened...but I love you." His lips quirked upward. "It may be too soon for you—"

"I love you, too," she blurted and then laughed at his stunned reaction. "I don't think either of us can explain what has happened between us." Sydney traced her finger across his lips. "I'm just glad it did."

Jett crushed her body against his and poured everything he had into her and prayed that it was enough. Finally, after a lifetime of seeking, he'd found love and he could honestly say that it was a love worth waiting for.

At 0700 hours Monday morning, Major Delsanto marched before his squad droning on the importance of the last leg of the Mission Employment phase.

"The ME phase includes seven flying windows called Vuls, showcasing bomber, transport, command and control, and refueling." Delsanto stopped and folded his arms. "You will be working with space operators, intelligence officers, special operations and air operations center personnel to test your newly gained skills. Each of the flying Vuls are meticulously managed by ME experts. These instructors are responsible for the scenario development, planning and execution of the Vul. Their attention to detail will ensure the Vul's cradle-to-grave process is executed flawlessly, and all training objectives and tactical problems are presented."

Adrenaline rushed through Sydney as she mentally prepared herself. The ME phase was the most difficult exercise. There would be no room for error—which meant she had to keep her mind off her husband.

No sooner had she commanded her thoughts than her gaze drifted over to Jett. He was more handsome and striking than ever. *And he's all mine.*

As if he heard her mental declaration, Jett cocked his head and winked at her.

Delsanto marched again and this time stopped before Sydney. "Keep your mind on your job," he commanded everyone, but Sydney took the message as personal and she forced her attention to the major before her.

"This course is designed to expose each of you to real-world situations our forces have faced in recent conflicts. The lessons you learn today could save lives tomorrow."

Silence met his words but excitement hummed among the anxious airmen like the strings of a finely tuned instrument.

"All right, everyone, suit up."

Dismissed, the airmen stepped out of their uniformed line and headed for the locker room. Sydney attempted to steal one last look at her husband, but instead her line of vision was blocked by Captain Trenese Post's solemn figure.

"We need to talk," Niecy said.

Certain she knew the subject Niecy wanted to discuss, Sydney turned away as a way of dismissing her. "There's nothing to talk about." She pushed through the ladies' locker room and made a beeline to her locker.

"Oh, I think we have plenty to discuss."

Sydney's annoyance escalated as she rotated her lock's combination numbers. "Look," she began, straining to keep her voice under control. "I appreciate you wanting to protect me and all, but I'm a big girl and I can take care of myself." Sydney's lock popped open and she jerked open the locker.

Unfazed, Niecy moved around to Sydney's right side. "So you're dating him anyway?"

"That's none of your business," Sydney snapped.

"I'll take that as a yes. Have you slept with him yet?"

Sydney wrenched toward the captain with her entire body burning for a fight. Before she could rip into the woman, Niecy held up her hands in surrender. "I'm going to take that as a yes, too."

"I don't give a flying—"

"Did your new *lover* tell you about the pool he and the guys had on you?"

The sensors in Sydney's brain short-circuited and went blank. Next, her knees folded as she awkwardly collapsed on a nearby bench. "What pool?" she asked, her voice low with dread.

Niecy sat beside her. Though her features held compassion, there was a hint of "I told you so" lining her eyes.

"Tell me everything."

Jett didn't realize he was humming as he suited up for the day's exercise, but Weasel and Lieutenant Blocker were quick to point out the phenomenon to him.

"Was she that good?" Weasel asked, leaning against the locker next to Jett's. "Any details you want to share?"

Jett's mood blackened as he slammed his locker. "You'd better not be referring to what I think you're referring to," he threatened.

"Ooh," the men chorused, and more men gathered around.

"You know, since you never actually tossed your money into the pot, you sort of disqualified yourself," Weasel said. "Of course, after seeing you and Serious together at Rain a month back, I took the liberty of placing my money on you. Easiest money I've ever made. I guess I should do the right thing and split it with you. I mean, you did do all the work."

The pool. I forgot about the pool.

"Look guys, I was never serious about joining any pool."

Weasel laughed. "Fine. More money for me." He slid an arm around Jett's shoulder. "But you could at least tell us whether the old ball breaker was even worth it. I bet double or nothing that Serious likes to be on top."

Like a starved lion released from its cage, Jett had Weasel laid flat on his back with his arm twisted behind him. A little more pressure and the limb would have snapped like a toothpick. "You're never to talk about my *wife* like that again. You hear me, asshole?"

Weasel sputtered and tried to wiggle free.

"I'll break it. I swear to God, I'll break it."

"Hey, man. Ease up." Lieutenant Blocker tried to step in. "Nobody knew you two got hitched. We were just teasing."

"Yeah, yeah, man," Weasel panted while he still writhed on the floor. "I didn't know you two were that serious."

Jett's grip on Weasel's arm remained tight until he heard the magic words.

"I promise I won't talk about your wife like that again. All right? I promise."

Grudgingly, Jett released Weasel's arm and stepped away from the man.

A few of the other guys helped Weasel up. The moment Weasel's feet touched the floor he crazily tried to attack Jett.

Happy to meet the challenge, Jett launched

forward. However, the rest of the squadron grabbed both men and pulled them in opposite directions.

"I'll get you for that," Weasel hollered.

"Bring it on. Let him go!" Jett commanded.

"You two stop it," Lieutenant Blocker barked. "You're acting like a bunch of teenagers. We're supposed to be suiting up for training. We don't have time for this."

When Jett realized Blocker was right, he stopped struggling. Fighting could easily get him kicked out of the program and he'd come too far to screw this thing up now.

"Let me go," Jett said calmly.

"Yeah, let me go," Weasel intoned.

Neither was released.

"You guys are going to behave?" Blocker asked.

"Considered it squashed," Jett promised.

After Weasel echoed the sentiment, the men released them.

Jett and Weasel glared at each other for a few minutes longer, but then snatched up the rest of their gear and marched out of the locker room. Though the quarrel was over, Jett remained upset about the whole incident. The voice in his head badgered and condemned his part in what had happened.

Across the room, Lieutenant Johnson slammed his locker shut and stormed out.

The fact was, Jett had agreed to participate in the pool, though at the time his intention had been to keep the overly testosterone-charged jerks away from Sydney.

Would she see it that way?

Guilt and doubt pricked his conscience. He *knew* she wouldn't see it that way. One thing was for sure: he would have to tell Sydney about the pool before another airman, mainly Weasel or Johnson, dropped the bomb on her.

That would be disastrous.

Jett drew a deep breath. This was not the way to start a marriage. He headed toward his assigned hangar and caught a glimpse of Sydney's curvaceous figure as she walked toward the same place.

He waited until she spotted him before he made a two-finger salute, but his feet slowed when he caught sight of her swollen eyes and angry face before she jerked her gaze away.

Jett frowned in concern, but in the next second noticed Niecy marching toward her. Niecy boldly met his gaze and shook her head. In that instant, Jett knew Sydney had already learned about the pool.

His heart sank at the realization that his marriage was in serious trouble.

Chapter 23

In a typical Red Flag exercise, friendly Blue Forces engage hostile Red Forces in combat situations. Blue Forces are made up of a variety of units from Air Mobility to Marine Corps. A Blue Force commander who orchestrates the employment plan leads them. Red Forces are composed of Red Flag's Adversary Tactics Division flying the F-16s and providing air threats through the emulation of enemy tactics. They are often augmented with other U.S. Air Force, Navy and Marine Corps units flying in concert with electronic ground defenses and communications and radar-jamming equipment.

Jett wasn't in the sky more than ten minutes

before the Red Force had a lock on his plane and eliminated him and his wingman from the competition. Sydney's concentration apparently was better than his, and she and Captain Post went on to run perfect circles around the Red Forces and complete their mission.

By the time Serious Garrett landed her jet there was no question among the squadron on just who would complete the nine-week combat training as top gun.

Meanwhile, Jett had returned to being that caged lion, pacing and waiting for the opportunity to tell Sydney his side of the story. However, Sydney went out of her way for the rest of the day to stay the hell away from him.

Captain Post had no such agenda. "I have to admit that even for you this was pretty low."

"You got it all wrong," he seethed, ready to defend himself to someone—anyone.

"Sure I do," Niecy hissed and started to walk away.

Desperate, Jett cornered her before she was able to slip back into the women's locker room. "You have to tell her I didn't make that bet."

Niecy's head rocked back with laughter.

Jett glared at her and waited until she was through. "I love her, Niecy."

She folded her arms. "I care."

"Goddamn it, Niecy. I mean it. This isn't like…"

"Isn't like what?" Niecy challenged. "Like all the other women? Like my other friends?"

He huffed in frustration. He wasn't going to get anywhere with her. He would be better off waiting for Sydney to calm down. "Just forget it." He turned away.

Niecy raced around him and blocked his escape. "I never could figure out guys like you. Do you get some kind of high from hurting women?"

Jett's frown deepened. Never in his life had he intentionally hurt anyone and he didn't know how to go about explaining anything to someone who'd made up their mind without all the facts. "No," he answered simply and stepped around her.

True, after Valerie had run off and married his brother he'd gone through a period where he sought solace in other women's arms. At no time did he lead anyone on. In the past, he'd made it clear he wasn't looking for a relationship—but there was no shortage of women who thought that they could change his mind.

Those were usually the ones he left brokenhearted.

"Just stay the hell away from her," Niecy shouted at his back.

Jett stopped in his tracks and then slowly turned back to face her. "Sorry, I can't do that, either. She's my wife."

At that admission, he watched Niecy's smug expression crumble before he walked away again.

Jett tried to give Sydney her space but after three days and more than thirty calls to Sydney's cell phone, Jett decided to hammer on his wife's door until she spoke with him. Nearly everyone on her floor expressed harsh comments at the amount of noise he kept up.

"Sydney, I know you're in there," he shouted through the door. "I'm not leaving here until you talk to me."

"You'll leave if I call the Security Police," another neighbor threatened.

"You hear that, Syd? Do you want to read about this domestic dispute in the Nellis *Bull's-eye* newspaper?"

Silence greeted his threat.

Jett sighed and slumped against the door. "Please, Sydney," he murmured, sounding like the broken man he was. "Hear me out."

Sydney stood on the other side of the door with tears streaming down her face. For the past hour she'd kept her hand on the doorknob, but had been unable to summon the strength to actually open the door. The pain she was experiencing threatened to tear her in two.

She just needed more time to sort things out, but Jett was determined to rob her of that time. If she opened the door, what would he say? What *could* he say?

He'll deny everything, the voice in her head warned. It was the only thing he could do. If he denied it, what then? They were married, for Pete's sake. Was that part of the pool, too?

Sydney shook her head. That didn't make sense.

"Sydney, please," Jett begged.

"Please," she whispered. Her hand tightened on the door, but she still couldn't do it. "Please go away, Jett."

There was a long pause before Jett replied, "I can't. I love you."

Sydney closed her eyes in anger as much as disappointment. With one burst of courage, Sydney wrenched open the door. "If you loved me how could you—?"

Jett flew into the apartment, wrapping his arms around her and smothering her lips with a ravenous kiss. The fact she'd opened the door filled him with hope. For a few wonderful seconds, Sydney's body went limp in his arms and she returned his kiss, then she pushed at his chest. When her efforts proved futile, she started swinging—first with open hands and then with tightly clenched fists.

Jett's lips tore away from her sweet mouth so he could dodge her vicious blows. More than a few of her punches found their mark across his jaw and cheeks as well as his chest and arms. "Syd…Sydney…stop!"

"You asshole! How could you do this to me?" She landed fresh blows against his temples that literally had him blinking away stars. Before he knew it, they had fallen to the floor—him wrestling her to pin her arms down and her trying to kill him.

"Sydney, you don't understand. I didn't participate in the pool."

"Liar!" She swung again and hit him dead in his mouth.

Jett was almost certain the woman had three hands the way she kept landing blows after he was certain he had her pinned. "Let me explain."

"What's there to explain if you didn't do anything?" she screeched.

He struggled with that one for a moment. "Okay, I should have told you about the pool, but the truth of the matter is I'd forgotten about it."

Sydney stopped struggling, and Jett eyed her wearily. Was this a real truce?

"You forgot?" she asked. Her chest heaved in exhaustion.

"I know that may be hard to believe, but it's the truth. Lieutenant Hawley told me about the pool nearly two months ago and well, I guess technically—or initially—I said that I was in—"

"So you *were* in on the pool?" She freed her hands and another round of punches landed upside his head.

Jett discovered that his wife was not only fast, but she was incredibly strong. Yet the fear of losing the best thing in his life kept him in the game. Somehow he had to get her to hear him out.

After another five minutes of wrestling, he managed to lock her hands above her head. By that time, they were exhausted. The anger in Sydney's glare scared Jett as nothing ever had before.

She doesn't love me anymore.

Instead of explaining, Jett kissed her again. He had to do something to erase the hate glimmering in her eyes. He had to get things back to how they'd been when they'd left the casino.

Back to when she'd said she loved him.

His kiss turned hard. He ignored her attempts to twist away. He even ignored the few times she managed to bite and draw blood.

She loved him—she'd said so.

Jett released her hands but then ripped open her shirt and broke the straps of her bra so that he could fill his greedy hands with her breasts. Sydney's hands flailed at him, but he knew she loved things rough.

Hadn't she said so?

He abandoned her lips and shoved a hard nipple into his mouth. He feasted like a starved man and took her writhing and trembling body as a sign she was just as turned on as he was.

He loved her. He had to make her see it; he had to make her *feel* it.

Jett tore at his own clothes and ripped them off in record time. He dodged a few more blows to press his lips back against hers. Their tears blended, and he swallowed her gasp as he pushed inside her.

"I hate you. I hate you," she rasped against his lips.

"No. You love me," he corrected as he deepened his thrust. "Say it," he ordered. "Say you love me."

Sydney thrashed her head, but her pounding fists flattened into gentle caresses against his back and shoulders.

"You love me," he insisted. "You love me."

"No." Her hips no longer resisted his rhythm but eagerly met his thrust for thrust. "No."

She was lying; he knew it and decided to teach her a lesson. By some miracle, he stopped his wild thrusting and held back. However, the feel of her vaginal muscles pulsing around his shaft was enough to dangle him over the pool of insanity.

Sydney groaned and wrapped her legs around his hips—desperate for him to finish what he'd started.

"Say it," he half ordered and half begged.

Tears splashed from her eyes as she shook her head, but she continued to thrust her hips in contradiction. Her head and her body waged a war and Jett, stiff and ready to explode, was caught in the crossfire.

"Say it," he commanded in a voice he didn't recognize. "Say it." He was no longer able to control his body and his hips moved again. He watched in glorious ecstasy as Sydney's eyes rolled to the heavens.

Sydney wanted to say the words—needed to, but the feel of her husband hammering away robbed her of the ability to talk. All she could do was feel, and what she was feeling scared the hell out of her.

Pleasure rippled across her body, then the sensation intensified until it became tidal waves crashing all around her. She gasped and dug her nails into the tender flesh of Jett's back.

"Say it. Say it," Jett urged.

The tide had made it to her eyes and caused more tears to stream down her face. An explosion erupted in her core and her body shook with violent tremors that caused her to hold on to Jett for dear life. Her mouth moved and formed the words *I love you,* but her voice was still M.I.A., so Jett never heard what he needed to hear.

Shortly after her mind-bending orgasm, Jett trembled and his breathing became erratic. Sydney knew his explosion was at hand. She discovered some reserved energy and kept meeting his hips to drive him over the edge. Through the mesh of her lowered lashes she watched his face contort and his jaw tense and relax.

She wanted to believe she was giving him something that no other woman could. She needed to believe their time together had not been a lie.

But he'd admitted to participating in that damn pool—a pool to get her into bed. Had the stakes been double or nothing to get her to walk down the aisle? Hell, it hadn't been like a *real* wedding. An Elvis impersonator had performed the ceremony, for Pete's sake.

Now that she had regained her ability to think

she wished she hadn't. Sydney Garrett was not used to feeling out of control, yet ever since Jett Colton had entered her life, it was her constant state of being.

Jett delivered a final thrust with a loud growl and trembled inside and outside her. He held her as if he was afraid to let go, but as his weight grew increasingly heavy, she finally pushed at him to get off.

Reluctantly, he rolled onto his side and attempted to pull her close, but she moved out of his reach. Sydney sat up and glanced around, suddenly ashamed of how they'd behaved liked wild animals.

"Syd—"

"This isn't a problem that you can just screw away," she said.

He sighed and sat up, as well. "I know that."

"This isn't going to work, you know." She refused to meet his gaze. "We don't know each other."

"You're wrong about that." He reached over and glided a finger down the valley between her breasts. "I think we know each other very well."

She recoiled from him as if disgusted by his touch. "Sex isn't a marriage. And I can't stay married to someone I don't even like." She glanced up in time to catch him flinch. Had she successfully hurt him as much as he had her?

She hoped so.

Sydney forced herself off the floor and walked nude over to the door. "I want you to leave. I'll start the annulment or divorce proceedings after the graduation ceremony."

"Syd—"

"End of discussion," she snapped and lifted her chin. She was back in control.

Jett locked gazes with her and tried to read her. After a long stalemate, he snatched on most of his clothes and marched toward the door with his shoes in his hands.

Sydney opened it for him and when he'd cleared the threshold, she slammed it closed.

Chapter 24

Once she'd slammed the door behind Jett, Sydney crumpled to the floor with her heart shattered into a million pieces. *Soldiers don't cry.* Her head repeated her personal creed, but soon her wrenching sobs drowned out its stringent order. At this moment, she wasn't a soldier. She was a woman.

And a wife.

"I hate him. I hate him," she croaked, mopping her face. Yet, as she said the words, she knew it wasn't true. But maybe if she said it long enough it would become true.

Maybe.

Twenty minutes later, she gave up and cursed herself for being so damn weak and gullible. How long had she prided herself on not being another fairy-tale-chasing, husband-obsessing single woman? Sure, she'd had her share of heartbreak in the past, but never anything that could break her.

Nothing like this.

Did James Colton truly love her?

As if on cue, Sydney's body throbbed and tingled with the all-too-recent memory of how he'd just made love to her. Hadn't she tasted his desperation? How many times had he told her that he loved her?

Why would he say that now, after she knew about the pool? The jig was up. He could've just walked away.

Then again, maybe the desperation was her own? She'd wanted Jett and she'd gone after him. So, maybe she'd got exactly what she deserved.

That thought was followed by another wave of tears. Pain radiated from where her heart used to be. Sometime later, she managed to peel herself off the floor and carried her solo pity party to the shower. There she hoped to wash away her husband's scent and touch from her body. However, it was an impossible task. Somehow, Jett Colton had branded her. And, as Sydney curled into the bed for the night, she wished fervently she'd done the same to him.

There would be no annulment—no divorce.

Sydney Garrett still wanted and loved her husband. In some way they would work things out.

At least she hoped so.

Jett cursed a blue streak all the way back to his dormitory. He cursed Weasel, nosey Niecy and all the men in his squadron for coming up with such a childish pool in the first place.

Then at last, he cursed himself.

After so many years, he'd found love and somehow screwed it up. His thoughts roamed to his impossible father, his elusive brother and his mysterious mother. None of them had been able to give him what he desperately needed.

It had taken a lifetime to create and become the cocky, hotshot fighter pilot with the love-'em-and-leave-'em attitude. Walking around with your heart on your sleeve was like walking around with a target painted on your forehead.

His family had taught him to keep people at arm's length, and the one time he'd ignored his own rule, he was back to square one.

"Damn!" He entered his apartment and threw his keys and shoes across the room. Neither action abated his anger or frustration so he looked around and found more things to throw. After a few minutes of this behavior, pounding resounded on the walls and door around him from his neighbors.

"Yo! Keep it down in there," a chorus of men demanded. "People are trying to get some sleep!"

"Go to hell," Jett roared, unconcerned about pissing people off. In fact, a good fistfight was probably what he needed. He could bear pain anywhere on his body…except in his heart.

Heartbreak left damage to the soul. Being honest with himself, he didn't know how he would recover from this. If he ever could.

Giving up his tirade, Jett collapsed on the edge of the bed and buried his face in his hands. For the first time in a long while, he felt like crying, but he fought the tears as vigorously as an enemy combatant. It was a fight he wasn't confident he'd win.

At long last, when he'd calmed his pounding heart, his thoughts obsessed on how he could fix this situation. However, every plan he came up with screeched to a halt when he remembered the pain and hurt in his wife's eyes. Eyes that could never forgive.

He stood up from the bed and headed toward the shower, walking like a man heading toward a lethal injection. Even a long shower failed to make him feel any cleaner. Returning to bed, Jett slipped beneath the covers with only one thought looping in his head.

Tomorrow Sydney will dissolve the marriage.

Sleep eluded him.

Shutting off the alarm clock before it had the chance to go off, Jett was not excited to face a new day—especially not one that was the beginning of an end. "I have to talk to her again," he mumbled under his breath, though he was clueless about what to say.

He had two hours before the graduation ceremony. Should he talk to her before or after? Jett warred with that decision for thirty minutes and then cursed himself for wasting time.

He pulled out his uniform blues and dressed. When he was finished he still didn't have a speech prepared. Jett could only think of one request. "Can you ever forgive me?" he asked his reflection in the bathroom mirror. He held his own gaze and wavered with his own answer.

After a long while, he lowered his eyes and leaned his weight against the counter. What did it mean if he couldn't even forgive himself?

Jett's shoulders deflated as he came to a decision. "To hell with it." He clenched his jaw and hardened his resolve. Even as he did so, the pain in his heart intensified.

He lifted his chin, met his gaze and took a deep breath. He would *not* beg for love again.

A knock hammered at the front door. *It's her.* Hope surged through his veins like a jolt of adrenaline through the heart. In four quick, long strides he made it from the bathroom to the front door. Jett didn't know what he was doing or that he was holding his breath until he snatched open the door. Surprise and disappointment hit him like a ton of bricks.

"Xavier?"

Jett's tall and handsome brother, dressed in a pristine naval uniform, nodded and waited.

Jett tensed. Something had to be wrong, but he couldn't bring himself to ask. He hadn't told his brother about his training at Nellis. He couldn't have—he didn't know where the hell he was, so the chances of his brother showing up for graduation were odds a mathematician would have trouble calculating.

He had, however, mailed checks to his father from Nellis. Had Xavier finally returned home and reclaimed his rightful place as the golden child?

Xavier drew a deep breath and glanced around. "Aren't you going to invite me in?"

Jett kept his gaze leveled as he stepped back and allowed his brother entry. The moment he did so the temperature in the room spiked.

"Sorry to drop in on you like this," Xavier began in a thick voice. "I'm sure my visit is sort of a shock."

Jett closed the door and turned toward the spitting image of his father. "You could say that."

The brothers stared at one another in an awkward checkmate for what seemed like an eternity.

"It's good to see you again, little bro." Xavier flashed his first smile, but it soon cracked under pressure.

"What are you doing here?" Jett asked, wanting him to get to the point. This sort of surprise made him nervous. "How did you find me?"

"The checks to the old man," Xavier replied, sliding his large hands into his pockets. "There were, like, four of them stuffed in his mailbox."

Jett flinched at the painful squeeze to his already bruised heart while dread seeped into his bones. "He didn't cash them?"

Xavier shook his head and then dropped his gaze to stare at his feet. "I finally go home…only it's too late."

Jett reached for a chair, trying to prepare himself for what he knew was coming, but Xavier said the words before he got a chance to sit down.

"Dad passed away. I need you to come home."

Sydney climbed out of bed without having slept a wink. All she had after a night of racing thoughts was a massive migraine. She toasted a bagel and swallowed four Tylenol tablets instead of the recommended two. Before the pills had the chance to work their magic, she donned her sweat clothes and hit the track for an early-morning run.

Maybe she could sweat Jett out of her system.

"I'll race you."

Startled by the gravelly baritone, Sydney let out a small yelp and then turned toward an equally surprised Lieutenant Johnson with his hands up in the air.

"You scared me," she admitted and then relaxed with a smile. "I didn't see you come up."

"Sorry. I guess you were in your own little world."

"I guess so." She resumed her light jog.

Johnson ran beside her. "Are you all right?"

Hell, no. My husband married me in order to win a bet. "Never better." She smiled and read in his eyes the truth. She stopped running.

Johnson also stopped.

"You know, don't you?" she asked.

He hesitated.

Embarrassment, shame and humiliation fused within her body and became a boiling anger. "So what do you want? Is there another pool to see who can make a bigger fool out of me?"

Johnson held up his hands again. "You're beating up the wrong guy."

She glared, but Johnson's sincerity unraveled her anger like a loose thread. "Was the whole squad in on it?"

"I don't know. I wasn't."

Their gazes remained locked until her head began to pound again and a new wave of tears stung her eyes. For someone who didn't like crying, she was doing an awful lot of it since Jett Colton had come into her life.

Jett pounded on his wife's apartment door for twenty minutes, begging for entry. He wasn't going to be able to attend graduation. He and his brother were booked on the next flight out to Georgia, which gave him less than an hour to settle things with his wife.

"She's not there," Major Post grumbled as she walked down the hallway and slipped her key into the lock two doors down.

"Where is she?" he asked, bracing himself for verbal combat.

Niecy opened her door as a sly smile slithered across her lips. "Down at the track...with Lieutenant Johnson."

"You married him?" Johnson asked, thunderstruck. "Are you kidding me?"

"What? Wasn't that also part of the pool?" Sydney responded sarcastically, but secretly wanted an answer.

Johnson blinked as if he was unable to process the information.

"It really doesn't matter." She shrugged and began walking. "The marriage is over."

After a few minutes lapsed, Johnson found his voice again. "Are you sure?"

Sydney hiked her shoulders. "How can it not be?"

"Well." He sighed. "I guess that depends on whether or not you love him."

She fell silent.

"Do you?" he asked.

"More than one person has to be in love for a marriage to work."

Johnson stopped walking. "How does he feel?"

He says he loves me.

"Have you asked him?"

Jett raced toward the track in his polished dress shoes fast enough to qualify for the Olympics. His heart and his head knew that Lieutenant Johnson was bad news, mainly because a person would have to be blind or stupid not to know Johnson had feelings for Sydney. Secretly, he feared that the lieutenant was more of a love match for Sydney than he was—he just hoped she didn't come to the same conclusion.

But that hope died when the track came into view and he spotted Lieutenant Johnson and his wife locked in each other's arms.

Jett stopped running and simply stared at the couple. He waited for the long hug to end, or rather for Sydney to push Johnson away.

That didn't happen.

What he saw instead was Johnson's head descending and his lips land on Sydney's upturned face.

So much for love.

Jett turned around and strolled back to his apartment with his head down and his heart shattered.

Sydney stood still as Lieutenant Johnson kissed her—more from shock than anything else. When he realized she wasn't kissing him back, Johnson pulled away and smiled awkwardly at her.

"Why did you do that?" she asked.

"Because I may never get another chance." He smiled. "I hope things work out for you. If not—who knows?" It was a statement and a question.

Sydney couldn't bring herself to answer. Not because she felt there was a possibility, but because she didn't want to hurt a friend.

He nodded, understanding her silence. "Good luck, Captain." He winked. "See you at graduation."

Major Charles Maxwell stood before the graduating class with his shoulders squared and his chin thrust high. At the sound of his voice everyone knew his speech was a well-crafted work of art.

"I am proud of each and every one of you. The course you have just completed was designed to expose you to real-world situations our forces have faced in recent conflicts. In completing the exercises you are now combat air force experts in tactical integration."

Sydney tuned out again and cast another glance around, searching for Jett. Her game plan was to approach him calmly and request that they go somewhere they could talk. In fact, she'd rehearsed a speech. She even promised herself to be calm, cool and collected, but with Jett's noticeable absence, her calm was morphing into panic.

Had he skipped graduation as a way to avoid her?

What other explanation could there be?

Lieutenant Colonel Bryant replaced Major Maxwell and another rehearsed speech was under way. An hour later, Sydney's patience for the whole proceedings was wearing thin. For the first time in her military life, Sydney found it hard to remain in perfect formation.

She was so absorbed in Jett's disappearance that she didn't hear her name called from the podium as the class top gun.

"Syd." Niecy elbowed her sharply. "They're calling for you."

Sydney blinked and heard the surrounding applause for the first time. It was enough to snap her back to reality, and she marched her way to the podium to accept her plaque and shake hands with the lieutenant colonel.

A speech wasn't expected, so she felt better for not having one. From the podium, she scanned the crowd and confirmed what she already knew.

Her husband was not there.

It was probably all for the best, she repeated to herself. The ceremony finally drew to a close and an endless line of congratulatory handshakes ensued. Sydney moved through the sea of people on automatic pilot until her whole body felt numb.

"There's our girl," Steven's voice rang out seconds before he enveloped his sister in his arms.

"As always, we're so proud of you," her mother announced, entering the fold.

Sydney had completely forgotten she'd invited her family to the graduation. It was just another sign that she wasn't herself lately.

"What's this?" Her mother lifted Sydney's left hand to stare at the simple silver band around her finger.

Sydney glanced at her brother who promptly averted his gaze by pretending to be fascinated by the weather.

"It's nothing," Sydney lied. "It's just a ring I found at an antique shop and fell in love with."

Steven's attention snapped back to her, but this time she ignored him.

"Sweetheart, you have it on the wrong finger." Her mother laughed. "For a minute you scared me. I thought you'd run off and got married or something."

Sydney laughed awkwardly but shot her brother a glare. "What would ever give you that idea?"

"Well, this is Vegas," her mother tittered. "Capital of the drive-through wedding ceremonies."

Sydney smiled. Should she search for Jett or wait for him to come to her? Should she file for the annulment or wait to see what fate handed out? Maybe this was one of those times when if you love someone you set them free. If he came back then it was meant to be.

"Why, I hear in some places an Elvis Presley impersonator will perform the honors. Can you imagine?"

Sydney slipped off the silver band, still unsure of her next move. "Actually, Mom, I can."

Escape

Chapter 25

Tuesday, July 4, 2006: 2200 hours. Somewhere in North Korea

Sydney lowered her Beretta and stared down at the dead body of the lone Korean soldier. He'd spotted her and aimed his weapon. Before she'd had time to think, she pulled the trigger. She expected the gunfire to echo through the woods and possibly draw more soldiers to the area, but instead the forest fell eerily quiet.

She waited for hours with a dead man at her feet. Then slowly her tense body began to relax. *Get up!* She struggled to heed the command; her bad left leg trembled like the last fall leaf on the first day of winter. Miraculously, she climbed to her feet and inched deeper into the forest. The farther she went, the thicker the trees became. She didn't select the place she would sleep for the night; it was more like she collapsed when she couldn't walk anymore. She curled up behind a thick bush and then extracted her radio.

"Anyone, this is Delta 6-6." She reverted to her handle, her identity still protected from enemy forces.

No response.

In fact, Sydney began to wonder if the damn radio even worked.

Sleep hit her like an explosion, but the night was entirely too short as the unmistakable sound of F-16 jets filled the sky.

Wednesday, July 5, 2006: 1000 hours. Osan Air Base

Combat Search and Rescue program is directed from the top by an organization called the Joint Personnel Recovery Agency (JPRA). The "Personnel Recovery" is the aggregation of military, civil and political efforts to recover captured, detained, evading, isolated or missing personnel from uncertain or hostile environments and denied areas. The moment Major Garrett's plane went down, the recovery operation automatically became a joint operation. Personnel from any service can be asked to assist.

Vice Commander Colonel Mickelson spent all night and most of the morning working with JPRA and both parties came to the decision to cross ten miles into the DMZ hoping for a signal from their missing pilot. Working with estimated coordinates from last contact with Major Garrett and from Captain Johnson's eyewitness account, Mickelson was confident his team would be able to make contact or locate any signal.

Captain Johnson made it clear that he wanted the assignment, but Mickelson chose to send the Black Knights back in. However, the carefully calculated chess move was apparently expected.

"Missiles in the air. Missiles in the air," Captain Colton transmitted before contact with four more fighter pilots was lost.

An explosion shook the ground around Sydney and her heart immediately leaped into her throat. Once the earth settled, another explosion followed and then another. As frightened as she was, hope managed to penetrate her veins. *They're here. They haven't forgotten about me.*

But then the world went silent again.

She glanced up at the sky, awed by the majesty of the trees surrounding her. Sydney turned the radio back on and scanned the lifeless channel for what seemed an eternity before despair evicted her hope.

I'm going to die out here.

The morning passed and the radio remained dead. She was exhausted, starved and dehydrated. By afternoon, she made a feast from leaves and figs—pretty much anything she could find. She stayed put, not wanting to come across any more Korean soldiers. The plan was to move only at night under the cover of darkness.

Sleep descended again before sunset. It was the same deep sleep that had claimed her before. When she woke this time, it wasn't to the resonance of jets or explosions, but to the sound of crunching leaves.

Sydney had another visitor.

Her brain instantly cleared and her weapon was back in her hand as she squinted into the silver streams of moonlight.

What she saw stunned her.

Sydney blinked, certain the image before her was a wild hallucination. The only problem was that each time she opened her eyes, the man before her remained the same. Her grip on the Beretta loosened, but she remained crouched and hidden behind the bushes.

Jett, however, doubled over and gasped for breath as if he'd just narrowly escaped the hounds of hell. When he finally brought his labored breathing under

control, he made a quick scan of the perimeter and
hunched down to pull out his radio from his vest.

All the while, Sydney couldn't take her eyes
off him. Either there was a glitch in her memory
or the past three years had been incredibly good
to her...husband. She lowered her gun and with
one hand reached for the silver band looped on
her necklace.

She must have disturbed the night's silence
judging by how fast Jett whipped out his weapon
and pointed it directly at her. "Don't shoot," she
ordered, but out of self-preservation she lifted her
firearm, as well.

For half a heartbeat an awkward stalemate
ensued before Jett's hauntingly familiar baritone
drifted toward her. "Sydney?"

Tears instantly burned the backs of her eyes but
she kept them from falling. If it weren't for the un-
bearable pain in her leg, she was sure she could
convince herself that this whole thing was some
supernatural dream.

Jett remained still while his eyes pierced the
thick bush in front of him. He'd recognized the
voice that had bade him not to shoot immediately.
However, a part of him believed his mind was
playing tricks on him. Had he actually found her?
And if he had—now what?

"Major Garrett, is that you?" he asked and
waited. Seconds that felt like minutes lapsed and the

small bush he kept his weapon level on rustled. Finally, she limped into the moonlight not unlike a Hollywood starlet stepping into the spotlight.

Jett gasped at the sight of the red, swollen burns stretching across the right side of her face. The left side was smudged with dirt and her lips were cracked and beginning to peel. Despite all of that, he was certain he'd never seen a more beautiful sight.

Sydney was alive.

He lowered his weapon and laughed with relief.

She lowered her gun and eyeballed him as if he'd lost his mind. She was certain at least one of them had. "Why…? How…?"

His laughter faded into a light chuckle as he stepped toward her. "I recently deployed to the re-established Black Knights at Osan. I'm a part of the combat search-and-rescue team."

She sighed with relief. "Did Captain Johnson…?"

Jett lowered his head. "Captain Johnson made it back safe and sound to Osan. You don't have to worry."

"But what's going on? What happened?"

"We're not exactly sure. Kim Jong-il test-fired seven nuclear weapons yesterday. We don't know what else they're up to."

Sydney's shoulders drooped under the pressure of despair and she whispered a quick prayer of thanks that Puck was alive and well. But there was something off about Jett's sudden appearance.

"Where is the rest of the team?"

Jett exhaled a deep breath and gave a solemn shake of his head. "We ran into unfriendly fire."

"Don't tell me the combat rescue team *needs* a combat rescue team, as well."

"All right." He sighed. "I won't tell you."

Sydney laughed at the absurdity of it all as she tried to ease herself back onto the ground. In a flash, Jett was at her side and sliding his hand around her stiff back. Just as quickly, her brain diverted from the intense pain throbbing in her leg but took note of the pleasurable warmth radiating from his body. Every nerve ending tingled to life as if it recognized its missing half.

Her gaze shot to his and she read in his eyes that he felt it, too.

"This isn't exactly how I pictured our reunion," he murmured.

Sydney's breath caught at the way he casually mentioned he'd been thinking of her. Their current predicament had a way of disassembling one's pride. "This isn't how I envisioned it, either."

Their gazes remained locked as so many emotions rushed through them, but instead of voicing what they felt, both decided to show it.

Jett's head descended through the moonlight like that of a handsome, mythical god from the heavens. Sydney slid her arms around his neck while her lips parted in anticipation of his kiss. When their lips sealed, time erased the past three years and the lovers had returned to the black silk sheets of their honeymoon suite at the MGM.

Now, as then, she couldn't get enough of his hungry mouth or his ravishing hands. The taste and feel of him was so exquisite, her tears came unbidden and rushed from the corners of her eyes. She pressed against him, wanting and needing to get closer.

When his lips deserted hers, she nearly cried out in protest, but his mouth returned to ignite a trail of fire down the column of her neck. Sighing, she rushed her fingers through the short crop of his hair. It felt too good to be back in his arms again.

Emerging from her haze of joy, she realized he was murmuring something into her ear. She struggled to concentrate and was soon able to make out his words.

"I never stopped loving you. I never stopped…"

Her entire body quaked and trembled at his confession, but the muscles in her throat constricted beneath the weight of her relief.

There were so many questions and too much to say; Jett doubted a lifetime was enough time to say it all. But, Lord, he could feel it. Even if she never said the words to him again, Jett knew she loved him.

The first sprinkle of rain was welcomed as a coolant to the blistering heat simmering between them, but as the fat drops quickened into hard sheets, he finally broke the spell to glance around for better shelter. Nothing readily met his eye. He could make a tent with the tarps rolled in their survival kits.

"Let's get a little deeper into the bush," he suggested and reached down to gather Sydney into his arms. However, her immediate yelp of pain startled him.

She pulled away and doubled over.

"What...where are you hurt?"

Sydney tried to answer but the pain in her leg was all-consuming and she could do little more than gasp for air.

Jett noticed the tourniquet wrapped around her leg and was nearly destroyed by the thought. The rain pounded them mercilessly and a decision needed to be made.

In less than five minutes, Jett had removed both his and her tarps from their survival kits and built a tent to protect them from the soggy ground and pelting rain. It was a rather big risk to position something so large and not quite completely sheltered by trees or bushes, but Jett was afraid to move Sydney until he was able to get a better look at her injury.

He switched on a small flashlight, but when he reached to inspect her wound, Sydney protested.

"No. No. It's all right," she panted, brushing his inquiring hands away. In truth, she feared that at any moment she would black out from the pain.

"I know it hurts," Jett said comfortingly. "But I need to take a look."

Sydney sucked in a breath and felt a fresh wave of tears rise. She'd spent the past twenty-four hours more or less just *wishing* away infection. Deep down she knew the truth—knew that the hot flashes she was experiencing could likely be attributed to a rising fever. If Jett inspected her leg, she knew her bubble of denial would burst.

"Syd, please. Let me take a look," he said gently.

Slowly, she removed her hand and glanced away. As Jett poked and prodded to get a better look, Sydney winced and ground her teeth. No matter what, she promised herself that she wouldn't ask him how bad it looked.

But what if it needed to be amputated?

At long last, Jett sighed and rewrapped his wife's leg. Since she didn't readily ask his opinion of the injury, he didn't offer it. After all, he wasn't a doctor—but he didn't need to be one to know she needed immediate medical attention.

"Don't worry," he encouraged with an emotional tremor in his voice. "I'm going to get you out of here." He turned off the flashlight and darkness surrounded them.

At that moment, she knew that if they were ever rescued, she would lose her leg. Jett started to move away, but Sydney reached and pulled him close.

"I'm—I'm…" What? Scared? Sorry? She licked

her dry lips and forced herself to be strong. "I'm so glad you're here." She buried her head against his broad chest and basked in the security it offered—even though she knew it was a false sense of security.

Jett's arms tightened around her as they lay back onto the tarp. For the longest time, Sydney remained still—content to listen to the sound of her husband's heartbeat and the rain. As the silence stretched, she realized that one of them needed to mention the huge question hovering over them: the past.

He beat her to the punch.

"Why didn't you ever file for divorce?"

Chapter 26

Why *hadn't* she filed for divorce? She must have asked herself that very question a million times in the past three years. She'd practiced some flippant answer if ever their paths crossed and she needed her best poker face. *I've been busy. I was waiting for you to file.*

Such answers were mind games. The same games she'd sworn once she wouldn't play.

"Syd?" he asked and then offered, "I can tell you why *I* didn't file."

"No." Tears fell with the rhythm of the rain. "I didn't file because…I didn't *want* a divorce."

Jett's arms tightened around her shoulders while

her confession hung between them. Her heart squeezed painfully during his ensuing silence and she wondered if it had been a good idea to sacrifice her pride.

Where does one draw the line between pride and love? She realized, with crystal clarity, that one destroyed the other. Hadn't pride prevented her from running after him these past three years?

Sydney burrowed deeper into the nook of his arms and wished she could gaze upon his features. But it wasn't safe to risk turning the flashlight back on.

"I know I said a lot that last night we were together. Most of it I didn't mean. I was just so…hurt. To the point that I wanted to hurt you back. I know that sounds childish—"

"There's not a day that goes by I don't regret hurting you like that," he said. His voice was like a warm blanket against the night's chill. "I had good intentions that got twisted and…"

Sydney placed a silencing finger against his lips. "It doesn't matter anymore."

Jett gently removed her hand. "I don't want it to be something lingering between us. When I said that I loved you, I meant it. I still do. I stayed away all this time because I knew you hated me. I didn't think that you could ever forgive…" His voice trailed off and for a long moment the rain seemed to speak for him. "Each day the divorce papers didn't show up in the mail, my hope grew. I just believed," he said, gathering his courage, "that if we were meant to be, our paths would cross again someday."

"And here we are." She half laughed and half sobbed. "So much time wasted."

"Do you…" *…still love me?* But again he lost his voice. Why was it that he always had to ask for love?

"I do," she whispered and carefully inched her body upward to steal a kiss. She was surprised by the salty taste of tears, but it only made her heart burst with more love. "I love you, James Colton. I will always love you."

"What about…Captain Johnson?"

Confusion clouded her eyes. "What do you mean?"

Jett searched her eyes. "I saw you with him…graduation morning…at the track."

It took a moment, but then the clouds cleared.

"He kissed me," she said, remembering.

Jett nodded.

"I didn't kiss him back." She held his gaze. "I don't love him. I never have."

Tenderly, Jett gathered her close and kissed her as he'd never done before. Their tears blended together and the world faded away. Controlling their physical urges became a true test of their military discipline.

The need to be truly reunited body and soul became an all-consuming desire, but Jett didn't dare. He couldn't and wouldn't chance further injury to her leg. However, Sydney was making it hard for him to refuse her advances. When it came to their relationship—their marriage—she regretted so much and she didn't want to regret this night if it turned out to be their last together.

Groaning, Jett wrenched away from her soft lips and then swore under his breath because of the pain of his erection. Here they were, lost in enemy territory, camouflaged and huddled in a makeshift tent in a heavy downpour, and all he could think about was making love to his wife.

Uncle Sam would be proud.

"Please, Jett," she begged when he continued to resist her. She peppered kisses along his chin and neck and slid her hand well below his waist.

"We shouldn't…your leg."

"We'll be careful," she promised softly—smoothly. "Please." *This could be our last night together.* She didn't know why that thought kept roaming through her mind—but it did. "Make love to me."

Despite their many layers of clothing, Sydney felt Jett's hardening erection in her hand and knew she was just inches away from getting what she wanted.

"We'll be careful," she whispered again and captured another kiss. "We'll be careful."

"We'll be careful," he agreed as his hands became jerky with need. He remained true to his word and took an extraordinarily long time undressing her. She didn't say a word, but he sensed that he still caused her pain when he removed the tourniquet and then removed her G-suit and other clothing from her body.

At one point, he heard her sharp intake of breath and a thick blade of guilt and stabbed his heart.

"We should stop," Jett said immediately.

However, Sydney could not be persuaded. Silently, she sat up and reached for him. At first, she just took his hand and slid it down the valley of her breasts until it rested on a chain around her neck. He felt the circular object and his breath caught. *Her wedding band.*

"I haven't taken this off in three years," she whispered and then pulled the chain over her head. "It's time I wore it where it belongs." She removed the ring from the chain but before she could slide the band around her finger he stopped her.

"Wait," he said. "Let me." In the next second, a small beacon of light beamed from the flashlight as Jett took the ring from her fingers. "We should do this right."

Sydney caught a flash of his smile and felt her stomach loop with knots.

"Sydney Garrett…Colton." He chuckled at the oddity of their marital situation. "Will you marry me—again?"

She drew a deep breath as her vision blurred. "Yes," she answered quickly. "I'll marry you as many times as you want."

Jett slipped the ring onto her finger and then took

her hand and placed it on his own necklace to reveal his own wedding band. "Looks like great minds think alike." He chuckled and then kissed her.

That was all it took for him to become lost in the touch, taste and feel of her. His clothes came off in a flash before he reluctantly turned off the flashlight. It was the first time their union had been sweet and tender. Neither one tried to become the dominant or the submissive. They moved as one. One body. One soul.

Thursday, July 6, 2006: 2300 hours. Osan Air Base

It had been more than forty-eight hours since Vice Commander Colonel Jeff Mickelson had slept. Judging by the constant stream of generals and colonels in and out of his office, sleep was going to remain an elusive memory for a while. Not only that, but the phone calls and faxes requesting situational reports kept his entire staff busy, as well.

The international community remained firm on downplaying the seriousness of North Korean missile launches—to the point that no mention of the missing American fighter pilots and jets had reached any of the media outlets.

To do so would have played directly into Kim Jong-il's plans.

Five years into the war against terrorism, the last thing the United States wanted or needed was to ignite a new war against a country with the third-largest military in the world—especially when China was their ally.

Could the world survive a third world war?

Another knock sounded at his door.

"Come in," he barked, without glancing up from yet another memorandum from the Secretary of Defense.

"Tell me you have something—anything."

Mickelson glanced up and then quickly jumped to his feet to salute Brigadier General Spencer Dugan. "No, sir. We're still searching, sir."

Dugan ignored the salute but waved Mickelson back to his seat. "We went from one missing plane to five in two days. We have to know something. The last thing we need is for this to become a crisis."

Mickelson was at a loss as to what to tell the general. Surely the man didn't think he was actually holding back information. "We're doing everything we can to find out who's responsible for launching an attack on our planes."

"With all due respect, we know *who* is behind the attacks. Nothing happens in North Korea without Kim Jong-il's say-so. The question is whether the surface-to-air missiles were launched from behind the DMZ or from within it."

"You think Kim Jong-il would be so bold as to infiltrate the DMZ?"

"He's bold enough to leave negotiations over his

nuclear program and then launch seven missiles as a *test*. So, yes. I think he would be bold enough to cross the DMZ. Of course, now, with our pilots forced to try and outrun heat-seeking missiles, they also crossed the DMZ. So we can't point the finger at the Koreans about the missing planes without them accusing us of crossing the DMZ first."

"Just the ammunition Kim Jong-il needs to say that the U.S. was provoking an attack." Dugan nodded and finally took a seat in one of the empty chairs. "Not a bad plan."

"From a madman—no." Mickelson braided his fingers. "As it stands now, our hands are tied. We don't know if our pilots are alive or dead. We can't risk another combat-and-rescue until we have pinpointed their *exact* location."

"And if we do locate them and perform an exfiltration, we can't get caught behind enemy lines. We need total denial ability."

"Which we won't have if our pilots are alive and are captured."

Dugan grimaced. "That would be a political nightmare."

Chapter 27

Sydney sighed dreamily as satisfaction hummed through her body. In the distance, the unmistakable soundtrack of birds singing and crickets chirping brought a smile to her lips.

"It's always a good sign when a woman wakes up with a smile on her face."

At the sound of her husband's voice, Sydney fluttered open her eyes and broadened her smile. "I see you're wearing one, as well."

Jett leaned forward and brushed a kiss against her lips. "That's because I made love to an angel last night."

"Anyone I know?" Her gaze drifted down and

she frowned. "Unfair. What are you doing already dressed? How long have you been up?"

He kissed her again. "A couple of hours. I cased the area and found a small stream not too far from here. I'd like to get you over there so we can clean your leg up a little better. I also found some good strong branches that I can fashion into a pretty good splint."

Sydney covered her immediate disappointment at Jett shifting to soldier mode. She was being ridiculous. They'd been shot down behind enemy lines and their primary mission was to survive, evade, resist and escape—not to mend a dysfunctional marriage, make love in the rain and whisper sweet nothings the morning after.

What was wrong with her?

Jett laughed as if he'd heard her thoughts and leaned forward for another kiss. "If it makes you feel better, I also ogled your naked body before I left this morning."

Unmoved until she met his stare, the woman in her won out over the soldier. "For how long?"

"For a *long* time." He laughed again and stole a second kiss.

Sydney slid her hands around his neck and deepened the kiss before she responded. "Then, yes, I feel much better."

When the morning smooching was over, Jett took extraordinary care in helping Sydney get dressed and repacking their tarp and camouflage nets. His guilt about their lovemaking returned tenfold when Sydney's attempt to walk on her bad leg proved impossible. Not only that, but her pride also returned in full force, and she refused to accept help.

After the blazing sun had zapped the rest of her energy and sweat was pouring like a waterfall down her body, she hitched onto her husband's back and allowed him to carry her the rest of the way.

At the surprisingly crystal-clear stream, she felt like and was certain she looked like a frightened deer. They were taking a high risk lingering to wash and clean up, because the area was so open. Both kept darting their eyes around in fear of being discovered.

Even with the two of them working on her leg, it took a considerable amount of time, and neither of them said what the other was thinking: infection had settled in. The splint Jett designed did aid in her walking, but the truth of the matter was she was beginning to lose feeling in the limb and her fever had returned.

"Try the radio again," Sydney said, unable to fathom how much longer she could survive out in the wilderness.

Jett nodded, but waited until after he had maneuvered her back into the thicket of trees and was satisfied with their hiding spot. He returned to the open stream and pulled out his radio. With little confidence Osan would able to pick up the signal, he switched on the channel, made a silent prayer and called for help.

Mickelson must have dozed off while he waited to be connected on a conference call to the president of the United States because when a loud rap sounded on his door, he nearly jumped out of his skin and his chair. His secretary didn't wait for him to bark his usual, "Enter," but rushed inside as though the devil himself nipped at his heels.

Annoyed, Mickelson shook his head at the young man. "Whatever it is, it's going have to wait. I'm about to take an important phone call."

Lieutenant Shaffer didn't bat an eye at the reprimand. "I think you're going to want to hear this, sir."

The young lieutenant successfully won his attention, and since the president had yet to come on the line, Mickelson leaned back in his chair and met the soldier's eyes. "What is it?"

"We picked up a transmission, sir."

Mickelson stood. "From?"

"Captain Colton, sir. We have a lock on his position."

Jubilant, Mickelson pounded his fist on his desk. "Hot dog!"

"That's not all, sir. There's another pilot with him. She's reportedly wounded."

"She?" Mickelson's heart clutched with hope for his no-nonsense, crack pilot who lived and breathed the air force.

"Yes, sir. Major Sydney Garrett is with him.

Captain Colton has reported that she will need immediate medical attention."

Mickelson nodded grimly.

"And…"

"And what?" Mickelson frowned at the young lieutenant's hesitance.

"Well, during Captain Colton's transmission he said something strange once."

Mickelson immediately thought that the captain might have been coerced in his transmission to the base and had wanted to warn of a potential trap. "What do you mean, 'strange'?"

Lieutenant Shaffer dropped his gaze for the first time and seemed uncertain of himself.

"Come on, Lieutenant. Spit it out."

"Well, sir. I could have sworn that one time he referred to Major Garrett as…" His gaze dropped again.

Mickelson was seconds away from throttling the young man. "Referred to Major Garrett as what?"

"As his wife, sir."

An excited Jett returned to Sydney's side and relayed the good news. Her reaction, however, was rather subdued—she flashed him a weak smile. "How long do you think it will take for them to get here?"

Jett's good mood soured at the sheen of sweat that blanketed her face. He placed his hand against her forehead and his heart nearly stopped. "You're burning up."

"No. It's nothing," she lied and slid her thick tongue across cracked lips. "It's just a slight fever." She attempted another smile, but it resembled a grimace. "How long?"

"Not long, baby." He brushed the hair back from her forehead. "The transmission was picked up on the Guard Channel. They know our exact location. You can hold on a little while longer, can't you, babe?"

She nodded. "Piece of cake."

Jett's eyes swelled with tears. The thought of losing her again after so much wasted time felt like a hammer slamming against his glass heart. Could life actually be this cruel?

A tear trickled down his face when the answer slammed into him. *Yes.* Life had always dealt him a bad hand. Why would now be any different?

Sydney slumped back awkwardly.

"Syd!" Jett caught her before her head slammed against a nearby tree. His heart lodged in his throat as he repositioned her and laid her flat on her back. "Sydney, baby. Wake up. Sydney." As gently as he could, he patted her cheeks, trying to wake her. When she didn't respond, he checked the dilation of her eyes and could barely contain his panic when all he saw were the whites.

"No. Oh, God. No." He patted her face again. "Wake up, Sydney. That's an order!" A sob escaped his closed throat as he scrambled to look around. He needed to get her cool or break her fever. Jett couldn't remember which.

His hands moved without much thought as he stripped off her survival vest, kit and G-suit. He also removed the splint he'd made for her leg. From her kit, he removed a knife and made strips of cloth from the suit. Next, he gathered them up and raced back to the stream to soak them in the water.

Hurry. Hurry.

It seemed he couldn't move fast enough. It was as if everything was playing in slow motion. *You can't lose her now. Help is on the way.*

He stood up from the water with the bundle of wet material, but when he glanced up, time stopped as his gaze crashed into that of a young Korean soldier across the stream.

One HH-60G Pave Hawk and two A-10 Thunderbolt IIs launched within minutes of Captain Colton's end transmission to Osan Air Base.

The HH-60G is a monstrous helicopter whose primary wartime mission is combat, search-and-rescue, infiltration and exfiltration. Recoveries are made through landing or rope-rappelling. The five-man crew consists of a pilot, co-pilot, flight engineer and two parachute jumpers. The A-10 Thunderbolt, commonly called the warthog or the hog, is a single-seat, twin-engine attack aircraft designed to provide close air support by attacking tanks, armored vehicles and other ground targets.

Now the team was airborne and covertly crossing the DMZ, the crew members staved off concerns about whether they could reestablish communication with the ground survivors. They stayed on the coordinates of Captain Colton's last transmission.

When they arrived at the evacuation site Korean soldiers were there to greet them.

The sound of heavy gunfire penetrated the hazy fog clouding Sydney's mind. Despite the steady pop of automatic weapons, the danger she was in didn't quite register. She could only think about how hot it was and how nice it would be to have something cool to drink.

After what seemed like a lifelong struggle, she managed to flutter open her eyes only to be confused once again by the jungle of trees surrounding her. As it had been after her last blackout, her memory was slow to kick into gear. When everything finally clicked into place, she forced herself into action.

But where is Jett?

Slowly, she sat up, surprised to be in just her basic olive-green flight suit. The shooting finally registered and she jumped to the conclusion that Jett had met hostile fire. Lying next to her was her survival vest and she withdrew the 9mm Beretta.

Determination overruled pain as Sydney lumbered to her feet. However, determination didn't stop her body's perpetual sweating. Realizing time was of the essence, she picked up her pace as she edged toward the sound of gunfire. If she were lucky, the element of surprise would be on her side.

The fact of the matter remained that she was unable to move swiftly, and she feared that by the time she did arrive, it would be too late.

It turned out that she *was* lucky.

An American soldier appeared seemingly out of nowhere and shouted through the deafening sound of the HH-60G hovering approximately a hundred feet above ground, "Are you all right?"

She nodded and nearly collapsed into the man's arms. From there, she had a devil of a time remaining conscious, but she must have been hoisted over the man's shoulder because the vision she had was of the ground and booted feet running across green grass. She blacked out, but came to when she was being clipped to some type of hoist.

Blackout.

Hands pulled her into the hold of a helicopter. At the back of the copter, another wounded soldier was being strapped into some type of apparatus.

Blackout.

"There's one more coming," a man shouted in the distance.

Sydney pried open her eyes and peered out a

small window to see a familiar figure race toward the lifting helicopter.

Jett.

She sat up, rooting like a personal cheerleader inside her head. But then she watched in horror as a Korean soldier closed in behind Jett and took aim. One bullet hit above Jett's knee. He stumbled and another bullet hit him in the back and spun him around to take a final bullet in the chest.

"No!" Sydney screamed, and this time she welcomed the darkness.

Epilogue

"Love is a fragile thing. You never know where you're going to find it or even when you're going to lose it." Sydney sniffed and then drew encouragement from the tightening grip on her hand. "The easiest thing to do is to take love for granted." She glanced up at Steven—her brother, best friend and diary all rolled up into one. "I'm sorry, I shouldn't be babbling on about this. What time is the limousine coming?"

Steven pressed back the sleeve of his black suit and glanced at his watch. "Don't worry. We have more than enough time."

Sydney nodded, but then removed her hands from his. For a long moment, they sat in silence while she composed her thoughts. "Daddy was the first man I ever fell in love with," she began. "For the longest time I didn't believe that anyone could ever take his place in my heart—so I didn't really bother to look."

Suddenly feeling foolish, she laughed at herself before glancing around her father's old private study. Her mother had kept everything pretty much the same. The grainy brown-and-white photo of her grandfather stared back at her. Underneath that one was a picture of her father, handsome and debonair as always. Next to him was her military photo. She'd stared solemnly into the camera determined to display the very definition of an air force airman.

Sydney lowered her hands and navigated her electronic wheelchair around the room to take a closer look at her picture. After a long inspection, she sighed and leaned back in her chair and chuckled. "I was so full of myself. I was always so..."

"Serious?" her brother supplied.

Her smile split wider. "Yeah. Too serious."

Her brother joined in on her amusement. "You're just now figuring that out? Appears I've been giving you way too much credit. I thought you were quicker than that."

She smiled and then turned her attention to the collection of model airplanes sitting on bookcases and shelves. "You know, I need to add a few modern planes. The HH-60G and the A-10 Thunderbolt II. After all, they did help save my life."

Her humor faded.

"Well, I'm sure we can find those models some-where—probably the Internet."

Sydney nodded, sniffed and tried to knuckle away a tear before it streaked down her face.

"No. No." Steven rushed up to her chair with his handkerchief at the ready. "No crying today." He knelt down beside her and gently dabbed her eyes. "It breaks my heart to see you cry."

Sydney glanced up at her brother while he fixed her face. Steven's strong resemblance to her father and matching baritone briefly transported her back to when he had said those very words to her and more tears rose to the surface.

"Okay. I think you've sprung a leak." He hopped up and rushed toward the door. "I'm going to get Mom."

Before she could stop him, Steven was out the door and she was left to fix her own makeup.

Less than a minute later, her mother gave a light tap on the door and then ducked her head inside. "How's my little angel doing?"

"Fixing my leaky pipes before Steven com-pletely freaks out on me."

As Bethany Garrett eased into the room and ap-proached her daughter, she held the same magnanimous smile she'd worn since the day Sydney had returned from Korea. It didn't matter what shape she was in, or how many surgeries she had to endure or how many nights she cried into her pillow from the one wound doctors couldn't fix, her family was just happy to have her home.

Sydney turned away from her mother and stared at the empty space next to her military picture. "There's another picture that should be up here."

Her mother placed a comforting hand against her daughter's shoulder. "I think you're right."

A knock sounded behind them and the women turned to see Steven enter.

"The limousine is here. Are we ready?"

Sydney sucked in a deep breath and waged a war against an army of tears. "As ready as I'll ever be." She shifted the remote and her chair wheeled around and rolled toward the door.

At the stairs, a newly installed electronic apparatus aided in Sydney's descent. In the foyer, her supportive family, including Uncle Billy, surrounded her and bestowed warm kisses and encouraging hugs.

It was a beautiful day. The grass was green, the clouds so white and the sky a beautiful blue.

Xavier Colton fidgeted in his black suit, trying his best to keep it together. His heavy heart was filled to capacity with guilt and regret. There wasn't much in his life he was proud of; there were plenty of times he'd let his younger brother down—too many to count.

But today, he was finally going to be the big brother he should have always been.

"The limousines are arriving," Valerie, his ex-wife and his brother's childhood love, announced as she entered the room. "Everyone is getting ready. Don't you want to go downstairs and greet the guests?"

Xavier hesitated.

Valerie moved to his side and slid an arm around his waist. "Stop punishing yourself. The past is the past. There is nothing we can do to change it."

He knew she was right. Jett had pretty much told him the same thing at their father's funeral three years ago, but there was something about the sadness and grief of his brother that day that had made it difficult for him to believe that he'd truly been forgiven.

How can someone forgive you when you can't even forgive yourself?

"Come on," Valerie encouraged. "It's time to do our duty."

"Duty. Honor. Courage. Integrity." Xavier smiled. "You're starting to sound like my brother."

"Those are code words for the United States Air Force. You forget, my father served." She winked. "Come on. Let's take our place."

As her black limousine rolled to a stop outside Atlanta Baptist Church, Sydney was nearly a basket case. She was feeling so many emotions at one time she didn't know how she could possibly go through with this.

"We can have the driver go around the block a few times if you need more time," Steven whispered in her ear.

"No." She shook her head and drew a few more deep breaths to calm her nerves. "I'm ready to do this."

They shared a brief smile before Steven lovingly blotted a tear from her face before it streaked down from her eyes. "Don't cry."

She nodded and watched as he turned and climbed out of the limo. In the brief moment it took for him to make it around she managed to wrangle a better control of her jittering stomach. The driver opened her door and she noticed he'd extracted her wheelchair from the trunk.

"That's not going to be necessary," she said, accepting her brother's arm. "I'm going to walk in there on my own two feet."

This time when she glanced back at her brother, tears shimmered in *his* eyes. "Shall we?"

"We shall."

Ever so slowly, they walked toward the church doors. When they reached the top stair, the door swung out and the "Wedding March" began.

Jett sucked in a deep breath at the sight of his beautiful bride walking down the aisle. He was just as stunned as everybody else in the crowded church to see her without her wheelchair. Due to their injuries in North Korea, the past four months had been incredibly hard. Somehow the three bullets he'd taken had all missed major arteries, but because the air force medical staff was unaware of their marital status, it had been weeks before either of them was able to get word about the other. By the time he was able to locate Sydney she'd feared the worst.

And so had he.

As for Sydney, her leg had developed an infection, but the military doctors were able to remove the rest of the scrap metal from her legs and treat the infection before it spread. After three months of intense physical therapy, she was now able to walk down the aisle so she and Jett could have an Elvis-free wedding.

Jett beamed as he stared as his bride, and his chest swelled with pride. He spared a brief glance at his brother and best man and winked. He was happy his brother had accepted his invitation and hoped that today would mark not only the beginning of a new life with Sydney, but would also be a foundation for a new relationship with Xavier.

Only time would tell.

He returned his attention to Sydney and watched as she completed the last few steps to the altar.

"Who gives this woman to be married to this man?"

"Her brother and her mother," Steven answered and then placed his sister's hand into Jett's.

Jett instinctively moved closer at the sight of Sydney's tears. "None of those," he whispered. "Your tears break my heart."

Sydney's smile bloomed. "I certainly never want to do that."

Saturday, November 11, 2006: 1400 hours.
Atlanta Baptist Church

Sydney and Jett sealed their love and life with a kiss...for the second time.

Dear Reader,

I believe Sydney was right. Love is a fragile thing. You never know where you're going to find it or even when you're going to lose it. In this story she and Jett nearly lost it twice. I'm glad Jett found his unconditional love, but I wonder what the true story was behind Xavier's disappearance and whether Captain Johnson ever got off the sidelines and found his soul mate.

I started writing *Blue Skies* before the test missiles of July 4, 2006. I always believed such an event would happen and originally set the story in the year 2012. Imagine my surprise on finishing this story to have such an event happen!

Stop the presses!

Anyway, I hope to hear from you on what you thought about this story. Please come visit me at www.adriannebyrd.com or show some luv at www.myspace.com/adriannebyrd.

Best of love,

Adrianne

His
TEMPEST

Favorite author

Candice Poarch

To gain her birthright, Noelle Greenwood assumes
a false identity and plays a risky game of seduction
with Colin Mayes. But when her feelings become
too real, the affair spirals out of control.
Then Colin discovers the truth....

*Available the first week of June
wherever books are sold.*

KIMANI™
ROMANCE

www.kimanipress.com

KPCP0200607

ALWAYS *Means* FOREVER

DEBORAH FLETCHER MELLO

Despite her longtime attraction to Darwin Tollins,
Bridget Hinton rejects a casual fling with the notorious
playboy. But when Darwin seeks her legal advice,
he discovers a longing he's never known.
How can he revise Bridget's opinion of him?

*Available the first week of June
wherever books are sold.*

KIMANI™
ROMANCE

www.kimanipress.com

Can she handle the risk...?

daring
devotion

ELAINE OVERTON

Author of FEVER

Andrea Chenault has always believed she could live
with the fear every firefighter's wife knows. But as her
wedding to Calvin Brown approaches, she's tormented
by doubts as several deadly fires seem to be targeting
the man she loves.

*Available the first week of June
wherever books are sold.*

KIMANI™
ROMANCE

www.kimanipress.com

KPE00220607

Love is always better...

The Second Time Around

Angie Daniels

Visiting her hometown, Brenna Gathers runs into
Jabarie Beaumont, the man who jilted her at the altar
years ago. Convinced by his father Brenna was a
gold digger, Jabarie never got her out of his system.
Now he's on a mission to win Brenna's heart
a second time.

*Available the first week of June
wherever books are sold.*

KIMANI
ROMANCE™